Random Deaths
and
Custard

Catrin Dafydd

Gomer

First published in 2007 by
Gomer Press, Llandysul, Ceredigion, SA44 4JL
www.gomer.co.uk

Second impression – 2008

ISBN 978 1 84323 824 9

A CIP record for this title is available from the British Library.

This book was first published with the financial support of the
Welsh Books Council.

Printed and bound in Wales at
Gomer Press, Llandysul, Ceredigion

To Meleri,
for laughing on the journey.

To Tadcu
for teaching me that patience allows things to grow.

And, of course,
to the young people of the Valleys.

Chapter 1

It's not that I'm superstitious or nothing. It's just that magpies really do give me the shits. More than black cats even. 'One for sorrow, two for nits, three for bird flu, four for shits . . .' I mean I keep on nearly crashin' my bike 'cos I've got one hand on the handlebars and the other one salutin' the black-and-white bastards. But no way am I really superstitious. Right?

It's just that I've started seein' deaths everywhere. My deaths. It's all a bit random really. And I'm getting all paranoid an' everythin', thinkin' I'm in a film with the Grim Reaper or somethin'. The weird thing is I've never been one to think about death before, like. So it's not a joke when you find out that you could 'ave died loads of Random Deaths, is it?

Anyway, my name's Samantha. I can't be arsed with introductions so that's all you're 'avin. And I'm not mad.

I live with Mam and Nanna. Nanna's mad. I don't mean it like that. It's just that she is a little bit mad. She hasn't always been mad. Just since Dad left really. I had to go and get her the day before, right? I mean, I shouldn't laugh; I shouldn't even smile about it – but it is quite funny really. The old bat was standin' in front of the betting shop in town chattin' to a few of the locals. Nothing funny about that is there? No, I know. But see, she was only in her petticoat. Funny thing is, the petticoat was nice enough: looked like a dress I'd buy in *New Look* or somethin'. But that I'd never 'ave bought it, 'cos I'd look like a slapper. And now, my Nanna's wearin' it to the bettin' shop. Anyway, I took her home, went to get her skirt and her cardi and stuck her in the front room with a tape of *Pobol-y-Cwm* that I recorded for her the day before, and she was happy.

Nanna likes the Welshy stuff. I used to be able to speak Welsh, see. I was quite good in school: Set 3 for most things but Set 2 for Cymraeg. We 'ad a really funny Welsh teacher, mind. I 'member one time me and Elen wound her up so bad that she started cryin' in the classroom. I liked Elen. Even though she was from a Welsh house, she swore and stuff. Sorted she was, and she and me and Arse were really close. At least we were until Elen went to sixth form, and Arse and me left. Then she started 'angin' out with some Welshy-Welshy twats. She's goin' out with one of 'em still. Alun his name is. Works in the County Council, thinks he's it. But he's not. I only remember one good thing Alun ever did. I'd been given a bollockin' by some Gog supply teacher because I'd used an English word in the queue outside her room. She took me to the Pennaeth Blwyddyn, Mr Warner – sound as fuck he was, and I got sent back to class. When I got back, I heard Alun askin' Gogbreath what word I'd said in English. It was the word 'brilliant', she said. He whispered somethin' under his breath, and the supply woman said: 'Pardon?' She said 'Pardon'! Beauty!

'Pardon's an English word too,' he shouted out and she was well embarrassed. I don' know whether he did it for my sake or just to show off. But, anyway, why should I 'ave 'ad a bollockin' just for sayin' somethin' in English? I liked Welsh, but it just wasn' cool and I couldn' speak it as good as I do English. And, anyway, nobody speaks Welsh round here now. 'Cept Nanna, I suppose and the Welshy Welshies up the street, of course. Their mum is a Gog, mind.

My mam isn't a Gog. Mam is from Tiwdortown, just up the valley from our house. She doesn't go there anymore, mind. Her brother Martin went to jail last year for hangin' about parks with little boys playin' on swings. No one likes Martin up there now and Mam is scared that people don't like her either, which is a little bit silly if you ask me: 'cos your brother's a paedo, it doesn't mean that you are as well, does it? Does it? Mam is well too sensitive. Takes everythin' to heart, worries too much. Anyway, I went with her to the surgery last week after work to get Nanna's prescription, and that's when I nearly experienced my first Random Death.

No one saw it, only me. I tried to tell Mam but she was too busy searching the bottom of her bag for the leaflet that showed that Nanna was Dad's mam, so that she could fetch her tablets. This is exactly how it happened, right? Imagine it like slow motion, like in a film and I'm Julia Roberts. Or, better still that I'm Marilyn Monroe or someone and the world is all black and white. I was crossing this narrow road and Mam was a little bit in front of me when I noticed that there was somethin' shiny on the pavement. Like a real magpie I was. I leant down to try and get hold of the shiny thing and noticed that it was like a silver cross or somethin'. As I bent down, I heard someone's reverse lights going off, a really pleasant and familiar sound. I looked up and slowly (and I mean very, very slowly) a milk van was reversing back towards me. I only just managed to get out of the way before it would have crushed me to death. I looked back to find the shiny object but I couldn't see nothing. It was as if it was a fuckment of my imagination. I know there's nothin' too amazin' about that potential Random Death, only it made me think, see. Could I have imagined the silver shiny thing so as to trick myself into an involuntary suicide?

When I told Mam in the chemist, a few people looked up at me (probably amazed that I was still alive). She just said:

'Don't be so fucking stupid will ew? The whole point of a 'suicide' is that you want to do it. You deciding to take your own life.'

And I said 'And?'

And she said 'And, you can't trick yourself into committing suicide, you silly mare! You've got to want to do it.'

By now a few people were watching us and listening.

'Yeah, but maybe my alter ego wanted to, see? Me, but not me, but me. Do you get me?'

'No, I don't.'

Then, suddenly, totally out of the blue, a girl pushed in between Mam and me and whispered,

'Will you please stop talking about suicide?

She was a bit pale, come to think of it, but still pretty enough. I smiled and said sorry and I think she quite liked my smile. People do for some reason. Maybe because my teeth are crooked; or maybe 'cos they know I mean it. See, I don't bother smilin' unless I mean it. D'you know what I mean?

Anyhow, my random end died a slow and painful death as I thought about it the whole way home with Mam. She was singing a Bonnie Tyler song and I was imagining my random funeral. No one would be wearing black because of the randomness of the situation. Somehow, I know they would have played a really cool pop song in the ceremony 'cos I was such a young and carefree person and then all my old school friends, who I don't even text anymore, would come to the stage and say some funny stories about me in school. We had a laugh in school. Two years ago now that was. Hard to believe isn't it? And now I'm workin', responsible and dyin' potential Random Deaths.

I would have liked to see people's faces when they heard what had happened to me. I would even be in the *Western Mail*, with a big picture of me. It's a shame you can't be around to be a part of it all really, isn't it? All your friends and family around and your uncles buyin' you drinks. Except Uncle Martin. Mam never let him buy us drinks when we were little. We were supposed to say 'No thank you' and run. But, sayin' that, I'm sure they'd give him a special day out to come and say 'Bye' to me. I tell you one thing for free: the people in work would love me. They'd have to close Custards for the day and have a trip to my funeral. The boss would have to say nice things about me and then they'd put a plaque up about me in the powdered custard section. 'Cos that's where I work. Mind, I just had a funny thought. One company who couldn't be in my funeral would be that milkshake company. Crusher. D'you get it? Crush Her. Oh fuck, I'm funny sometimes.

I think Mam misses Dad sometimes. I thought she was missin' him yesterday see, because I heard her yelping in the bedroom. A really mulin' sound, like a dog bein' squashed under a car. She sounded devastated and really lonely so I thought I'd go up and give her a cwtsh. She was screaming cryin', like a Banshee. I crept upstairs and got my laces stuck in one of the slits in the wood on the stairs. By the time I got up to her room, she was quiet again. I knocked and went in and found her lyin' on her bed watchin' *Coronation Street*.

'Are you alright Mam? You upset are you?'

'Aye love. It's horrible, just horrible.'

And I said 'Yeah, I know.'

'You don't tho' do you, *cariad*. Imagine being without the man you love.'

And I said 'Well, I can't even imagine bein' with him either really.'

'And imagine him runnin' away with a younger woman.'

And I said 'Come 'ere, I'll give ew a macca cwtsh.'

But she went on:

'And you bein' charged for murderin' that woman, when it wasn't even you.'

I was gettin' a bit confused now. Sounded like a very blatant way of breaking the news to me. So I said 'What do you mean?'

'Sacha here,' she said pointin' at the screen.

'Fuckin' hell, Mam! I thought you were talking about Dad.'

'Good God!' she said, 'why the fuck would I be cryin' about that bastard?'

So I left.

Mam did love Dad once mind. I know she did but she doesn't remember anymore. Or maybe she doesn't want to remember anymore. But, no matter what she says now, if I would have died my first milky Random Death, she would have been the first on the phone to him and maybe, just maybe, my Random Death would 'ave brought 'em back together. But it didn't happen, so tuff shit I suppose, innit.

Chapter 2

There was a funny story on telly today: George Bush had fallen off his horse on holiday. It would have been even funnier if the horse had fallen on him too! I reckon he's a twat. Gareth thinks so too – and Gareth should know. He's in Iraq, and 'aving a shit time. We had a letter from him the day before sayin' that he was homesick 'cos the food was so disgustin'. Bush made the war and now Gareth can't 'ave a decent meal. I think it's time he comes home now anyway, 'cos he's my only brother. He said he really missed mashed potatoes. I could never go long without mash. Never.

Mind you, I'm not sure if I actually miss Gareth. I mean, Gareth and me don' really get on at all. When we were little, he used to nag me to play Cowboys and Indians, and to climb up trees and things. But, even though I was a bit of a tomboy, I suppose, I couldn't be bothered. I remember one summer, I must 'ave been about eight, Gareth invited all the kids on the street to the back lane by the house. He even invited the Wilkinsons, despite the fact that they smelled like fish. God, come to think of it, that's an awful thing to say. But, that's what we used to say: 'Somethin' fishy on the way, somethin' fishy.' Anyway, Gareth had called us there to tell us that he was 'King of the Forest' – whatever that meant. I told him to stop talking shit. 'Yeah, prove it,' said someone else. Suddenly, he pulled a dead bird from his pocket. I put my hand to my mouth. I remember how shocked I was now. He'd grabbed it from a nest in the trees. A little, teeny-weeny bird. I told 'im he was sick, twisted even. He smiled. Looked guilty for a bit. And then threw the bird to the floor, before standing on it and smiling. 'Who's the king of the forest?' God, tha' was a foust thing to do. A really foust thing to do. And Gareth was so normal usually.

Anyway, I was sittin' there watching Sky, like I always do

when I come back from the factory, and imaginin' being in America, when Nanna came in. She sat next to me and farted. I don't mind farting at all but hers really smell 'cos she eats random things and her insides are old. I asked her if she'd mind goin' outside if she wanted to do that again, but she just kept on and on. I reckon she was doin' it for attention. So, in the end, I did what Mam used to tell me to do with my little cousin Ems when she cries when I put her down, to sleep like: I ignored her. And Mam was right. After a while Nanna stopped farting.

Old people bug me sometimes. Nanna breathes loud and breathes a lot and so you can hear her chest going up and down like an old cage door opening and closing. Anyway, she wanted to look at a programme in Welsh, so bein' as she's my Nanna, I let her – although I knew I'd be bored out of my skull. By mistake I flicked to one channel where a scientist was saying that the world wouldn't be a nice place for people to live in a hundred years if we carried on polluting the air with gases. I looked at Nanna and wondered what effect her gases were 'avin' on the planet. Then, weirdly, I changed it to the Discovery Channel and there were random facts about shit and shittin' on. Apparently there's this bass note that exists that makes anyone who hears it shit themselves. Please God, Nanna's not wearin' her hearin' aid when that 'appens.

I found the Welsh channel eventually and *Wedi 7* came on. It's like *Richard and Judy* but without Richard and Judy. I understand it all really, so I suppose I do still remember my Welsh. Nanna was smilin' watching the programme. Half, 'cos she was so happy that she was listenin' to Welsh and half 'cos she'd had a mischevious idea, so I went to get some more of her tablets. When I came back, the programme was live from Caernarfon. I remember I went up there with school once. It's bloody mad up there, mind. They seriously speak

14

Welsh to each other and they're not taking the piss. They actually probably say things in Welsh to each other when they have sex an' all in Caernarfon. That's mad that is! Innit? Mind you, when I told Maggie in work today that I used to speak Welsh, she was well impressed, so she made me say some Welsh things like '*bore da*' and stuff. Maggie told Chief and Chief told Penny the boss. She asked me if I wanted to translate some signs for her 'cos she didn't want to pay a company to do it if I could do it instead. I was translatin' 'Best Custard in Town' when it struck five o' clock, so I'll start again tomorrow. I wrote something like '*Y Cwstard Gorau mewn y Dinas*'. I think that's right. But I might ask the Gog woman up the road sometime. Just to make sure innit?

While we were watchin' *Wedi 7*, Tomtom came in and sat on Nanna. Tomtom's our cat. He gets ignored quite a bit but we love 'im really. A bit like Nanna, I s'pose. Perhaps that's why they like each other so much. Tomtom always chooses to sit on Nanna before me or Mam. Nanna doesn't make a fuss over him or stroke him. Tomtom's a Tabby. Pretty he is, but when I get my own place, I'm gonna get a black cat. Good luck all the time then. But for now, I'm happy with Tomtom – 'cept when he farts. 'Cos he farts too and that's a mankin' smell, I tell you. Hundred times worse than a human's fart, even worse than Nanna's, 'cos you don't know where it's come from and what the fuck he's been eatin'. Mankin'! Mulin' actually.

Then something really weird 'appened: I 'ad two text messages the same time. That's somethin' that really freaks me out, two people in the world thinkin' about you at the same time. The same bloody time. Anyway, I looked to see who it was. Maggie's name flashed up first. Chief's band, Death of the Sales, Man! were playin' Treorchy tomorrow

15

night, apparently, and she was askin' me whether I wanted to go up there with her. I could think of a million better things to do. Chief's our boss. He's older than Maggie and loads older than me, and I can just imagine the type of music his group would play. Shit heavy rock stuff. I can see it in his eyes. He's got anger to deal with. Anyway, I texted her back sayin' I wasn' too sure 'cos I 'ad to babysit Emma's baby next door, maybe. To be honest, another reason I wouldn't wanna go is because I know that one of the boys who used to be in the band died last year. Overdosed on heroin. I don' like the idea of 'angin' about with people who do tha'. I've been there, done that. Not taken drugs like, but I've seen what they do, and I can' be arsed to go through that again.

I looked over at Nanna who looked as if she needed some more pills. But I 'ad another text to read. I was quite proud of myself for answerin' Maggie back straight away. 'Cos texts are weird. There's like an unwritten rule that you don' 'ave to contact back straight away. If you do, that's mega nice, but if you don't, people don' get ofended. It's the same with phonecalls now too. I never answer my mobile. I wait for an answer machine and then text back. And I know that's what everyone does these days. Anyhow, my second text was flashin' green. A little envelope in the corner of the screen. I pressed the read button and there was a text from Arse. Well, bloody nora, I thought. Long time, no text. Askin' whether I wanted to come to Merthyr with her one night after work. She'd drive, got a new car. Fuck me, she's got a new car. Guaranteed, that's why she'd asked. She wanted to brag that she's got a new car. Well, that's fair enough. And anyway, I fancy goin' over Merthyr anyway. Just over the mountain. That new retail park place 'as opened. KFC, McDonalds and shit loads of shops. I'll never 'ave to go into the middle of Merthyr again. Thank fuck for that.

After watching *Wedi 7*, I went to the kitchen to fetch the pills and that's when I had my next Random Death. I couldn't believe it, and there was no-one there to see me or save me. I was standin' by the cupboards lookin' to see if we had any Fray Bentos in. I love the stuff. Gooey and crispy and everythin' in one little tin. 'Where's it to?', I was askin' myself while lookin'. Anyway, I heard a noise outside. I took my head from the cupboard and looked through the window: next door's dog was eating the food Mam puts out for the birds. Leftovers like. Mulin' stuff like the skin from Nanna's porridge and dry, flaky crusts from bread. I knocked the window and, as I did, the whole cupboard above the worktop fell from the wall. It was like an earthquake. It was 'orrible, really noisy and tins fallin' everywhere. Thank God for that dog, I thought, or else I wouldn't have been here to tell the story. I had just avoided my second Random Death. And it would 'ave been so bloody embarassin' too: 'Aye, that's right, aye, a cupboard full of tins, yes. Landed on her head, yes. Decapitated she was'. Mam would have felt so guilty too. I can just imagine her now. She'd feel so bad that she hadn't had the cupboard fixed. See, we've all known for a while that it was a bit wonky and it does do funny noises sometimes. Anyway, Mam came runnin' in, didn't she, givin' me a bollockin':

'What the fuck 'ave you been up to now? For fuck's sake, look at the bloody mess!'

I said, 'I'm sorry Mam. I tell ew what tho', you're lucky I'm still 'ere to tell the story. I had my head stuck in there lookin' for Fray Bentos two seconds ago.'

'Shut the fuck up with all that bollocks again, an' go phone Shane Harries's boy. O *Duw*, there's an awful mess 'ere. He better still do things like put cupboards back on walls.'

'Alright, but isn't he doin' time?' I asked.

'No, love.' Mam said, 'It wasn' 'im that killed 'er after all.'

I nodded and went to phone. I was feelin' elated, really happy, so glad to be alive.

Mam shouted again. She was in a foul mood today:

'Get Nanna some chips from Hoi Wan too, will ew? And keep her out of the kitchen. It'll shit her up and make her a bag of nerves.'

Bag of nerves, bag of nerves. I always thought that was a funny sayin' and 'for Pete's sake' too. Cos, I mean, who the fuck is Pete? We don't say that around here but I 'ave 'eard it on telly, like.

I went from the kitchen to see Nanna after phonin' Shane Harries's son. But when I got there, she was gone. I didn't tell Mam. I just went around the house to see if she was upstairs or on the toilet, but she wasn't. By the time I got back to the front room she was sittin' there, eatin' a bag of chips. She's not that stupid, see. But she hadn't bought me any. Selfish cow. She was eatin' a jumbo sausage too. I settled down next to her, ready for a night of sausage farts and Welsh telly. I hinted for some chips, but she never got the hint. But, for some reason, I didn't mind that much. After all, I was still alive wasn't I?

When I came back Mam told me she was sorry for bein' an arse all day. Apparently, my Uncle Martin was found 'angin' this mornin', on a tree in the woods up Tiwdortown. He didn't turn up in court this mornin' and then the police went lookin'. They phoned Mam to say, but I don't think she wanted to know really. He didn't manage it either, dyin'. I feel sorry for 'im really. He obviously wanted to go, if he tried. Or p'raps he just wanted Mam and other people to notice 'im . . . I might go up there some day.

18

Chapter 3

My bike 'ad a stroke recently. Just as well this morning, mind. It was going to piss down with rain any moment so I was glad that I had to take the bus. The bus gives you time to think. And this morning I was thinking that I'm sad as fuck. But then again, I'm sure most girls are.

I'd been on the way to catch the bus when I saw this boy I used to go to school with. Stephen 'is name is. I fancied 'im for five years on and off and when I saw 'im today, I smiled and said, 'aright?'. He smiled back. Maybe he actually fancied me too. Maybe he'd been too shy in school to admit how gorgeous I was! Anyway, he was in my 'ead so much that I was nearly convinced that he 'ad followed me on to the bus and was sittin' behind me. The crazy thing is, I knew this wasn't true. But still I was sure he was kissin' me on my neck and tellin' me how much he'd always liked me in school. Tellin' me he wanted to shag me, tellin' me all romantic things. He meant more to me than all my family for a moment then. I turned around to look 'im in the eyes, and saw this old man sittin' there. Fuck, I must be mental. It's a mulin' experience. When you dream in the day, it's more than a daydream, it's like reality.

Anyway, the bus passed Stephen on the way up to Custards. And I saw 'im meet someone. And they kissed. Fuck me, I thought, before blushin' for thinkin' that he'd fancied me. And then I saw who he'd kissed. It was a boy. Fuck me. Stephen always used to sit with the girls in school. I see why now. God, that's so weird, I thought. How you don' realise things like that until you're older.

Wet days and Cutstards don't mix. When it rains, the

factory windows steam up like hell and you get a horrible feelin' in your belly. I got to work early. I don't know why, I just had a funny feelin' I better. Nanna always said I was psychic. Of course, if I really was psychic, I could predict far better things than comin' to work early. Maybe I'm semi-psychic.

Anyway, on my way in, I saw Chief. He didn't look too 'appy.

'What's the matter Chief?'

'Nothin. Go to Hell!'

Could come true sooner than you think, I thought, but I didn't say nothin'. And he walked past with a face like a slapped arse. Moody bugger. That don't help no one, does it? Bein' a moody bastard. It just puts everyone else in a real bad mood too. Anyway, I didn't ask anythin' else.

I like lots of the people I work with in the factory. It's an alright kind of place to work. You get half an hour on lunch and the industrial estate is so borin', you are glad to get back to work. The company is alright with us too: 'Custard R Us', but we all call it 'Custards'. We get gallons of the bloody stuff Christmas time if we over produce and you can give custard to people like presents then. We've got custard in tins, custard in cartons. We've got strawberry-flavoured custard, chocolate custard and powdered custard (which is where I work). And we've got organic custard and wheat-free too, for the posh people in Cardiff. Have you seen the price on 'em? And they don't taste that nice either. To tell you the truth, funny thing is, I don't like any kind of custard. Custard turns on me.

Anyhow, today I was just mindin' my own business, translatin'. In fact, I've been bloody translatin' for at least a whole week, so I haven't done any proper work for a while. I thought I best tell Chief about this, but then he was in such a foul mood . . . So I thought I'd ask Penny. Penny's the big boss. Well, I mean, the big boss in the factory. She's alright but she looks at you funny when she speaks to you. She can never keep her eyes on your eyes. She wanders, has a look at what you're wearin' (which is the same bloody uniform each bloody day – what does she expect, a ballgown?) and then rests her eyes just above your eyes. In the end, I couldn't be bothered to ask her why I was still translatin' either. Thing is, I think it's an honour that she wants me to do an important job like this one.

I translated all day. '*Cwstard am pob amser y blwyddyn*' – 'Custard throughout the year'. That took me bloody ages. I might get into this translatin' malarkey. Mind, I don't know what the Welsh word for 'translating' is. Doh!

Anyway, after work I was cream crackered 'cos I'd been thinkin' all day. But worse than that, Maggie, who sits with me on the desk, has been talkin' about her problems. She's well nice, fair play. Really kind, really smiley, when you need her to be, you know? She's two years older than me, but she's a good friend, actually. Anyway, Maggie wasn't all smiley today, and I found out why after she came back from one of her fag breaks:

'I'm pregnant, aren' I.'

'I don't know, are you?'

'Aye,' she said, lookin' at me as if I was gonna say somethin' mind blowin'.

'Fuck. You OK?'

'Aye.'

We sat in silence for a while. I was strugglin' with a Welsh word – '*newid*'. After a while I asked her somethin'. I know I shouldn't 'ave, but I did.

21

'You gonna keep it?'

'Course I'm gonna fuckin' keep it! What d'you think I am, a murderer? For Fuck's sake. Ewer so fuckin' immature! Christ!'

Turns out she wasn't shoutin' at me really. She started cryin' after shoutin', sayin' 'Sorry, sorry' and spit was fallin' from her mouth and it was really embarrasin'. Turns out the question was a fair question to ask (that's what Mam said when I got 'ome) but Maggie explained that she was too far gone. Thing that had upset her most was the fact that her mum had called her a whore. Just 'cos she didn't know who the father was. There was a choice of three, apparently. How does that make Maggie a whore? If a man had three girls lyin' about everyone would think he was a legend. I tried to be a friend but she just looked at me and said,

'You're only 18 mun, you aven't lived yet.'

And what's awful is, the only thing I could think was 'Fuck me, I haven't lived and I nearly died yesterday, and the week before come to that. That would 'ave been a bit shitty.' And I felt really guilty for thinkin' about myself, but that's what you do all the time innit? I wanted to ask her who the three 'possibles' were. She said she thought she knew who it was, until this mornin' but that it's turned out she's wrong. When she said that she kept bawlin' and bawlin'. In the end I thought she'd 'ave to stop 'cos there wouldn't be more wet in her to come out. When she was cryin' she looked really, really ugly. Awful ugly, all red and puffed up. She's not the prettiest girl in the world when she's not cryin', but she looked bloody awful cryin'. Everyone was lookin' at her too. I told her I wouldn' mind goin' out with her some time, to chill out. She smiled. I told her I wouldn' mind goin' to see Death of the Sales, Man! if she really wanted. She cried more

22

when I said that and I reckon it was because she could suddenly see her freedom disappearin' down the drain.

That night after work I went to Tesco, only for quarter of an hour. I went there meanin' to buy *Heat* magazine. I thought I had to have somethin' to read, to take my mind off the stuff with Maggie. That was heavy-duty stuff and I wouldn't be able to sleep. I actually bought *The Western Mail* too. I figured I don't read enough so I thought I'd educate myself a bit. Truth was, I knew it would be really borin' and that I was just gettin' it so that Nanna could see when that Dai Jones bloke is on telly. I swear she fancies him or somethin'. Big fat bastard he is. Farmer. Anyhow, I was flickin' through all the mags, 'avin' a look at the ones I wouldn't buy too, when I felt a tap on my shoulder. I turned round fast and that's who was standin' there was Mrs Evans from school. In actual fact we always called her Mrs Mop 'cos her hair was all over the shop. She was sweet mind. Taught me Welsh in Year 8. Shit, I thought, I'm gonna 'ave to speak Welsh.

'Wel, a sut wyt ti? Ers sbel! Wyt ti'n iawn?' she smiled really genuine, askin' if I was alright. Awful thing was, she looked at my belly for a minute and I caught 'er. I swear she was wonderin' whether I've 'ad a baby yet or goin' to 'ave one soon.

'Ie, Miss. Fi'n dda. Ti?'

'Paid a' ngalw i'n "miss" nawr, Samantha,' tellin' me to call her Enfys now. Rainbow, that means. Weird name innit? I wanted to tell her I was translatin' in work but for some reason I couldn't. Worried she'd be surprised, I suppose. I didn't want her to knock my confidence without tryin'.

'A beth wyt ti'n gwneud gyda ti dy hun? Oes gen ti swydd?' Cheeky cow, 'course I got a job. She didn't mean it like that mind. I know she didn't.

'Ie Miss. Fi'n weithio yn Custards. Fi'n mynd pasd yr ysgol yn y bws bob dydd.'

Fuck, that took it out of me. But she was smilin', glad I could still speak Welsh and all tha'. She liked me in school, mind. She liked me because I told her once that *Morwyn y Dwr*, this book we read as a dosbarth, was one of the best books I'd ever read. That was true, in a way. 'Cos, I'd only read about another ten in all my life, plus *Morwyn y Dwr* was the first Welsh book I'd read that talked about sex. She was a nice teacher to everyone too. If I said somethin' in English, she'd try hard to make me think of the Welsh word. She wouldn' put me on '*ataliad*' or '*taflen*'. She'd actually try and work it out with me. And I suppose, that's the point innit. It takes much more effort to try and get a word out of someone than it does to chuck someone out the class. When Arse 'ad an abortion after her stepfather raped her, we went to Mrs Evans for help. One dinnertime in Summer it was. We were both in Year 10 and Mrs Evans was cryin' 'er eyes out without noticin'. I think she felt sorry for Arse. I know she wanted to ask about her today in Tescos. If she had, I could have told her some good news: Arse's Mam 'as got a new boyfriend now. Runs a scaffoldin' firm in Aberdare. Loaded too. Hence the fact that Little Miss Arse Hole 'as got a new car. Ah well.

I was glad Mrs Evans had stopped to say hello. I found out she has two girls, one called Cadi and the other called Morfudd or something. And she still lives down Cardiff way. They all do, don't they. I said ta-ra and I was sad to say ta-ra. I see loads of those wanker teachers in Tescos and they see me too, but they never stop. They never even raise their hand. Too far up their own arses. But she isn't. She's alright.

That night, after gettin' in from work, I wanted to chill out and get some things out o' my head. I told Mam she could go out to the Legion on the piss with her mates, and that I'd take Nanna and Anti Peg from Tiwdortown to Bingo. Nanna switches on when you take her to Bingo, she's like a new woman. She'd been in her room for hours dollin' up and Anti Peg arrived six o' clock sharpish. Anti Peg's a funny one. She's really unique. Mind you, I remember my teacher in school tellin' me that nothin' can be really unique. If it's unique, it's unique. Whatever. As I was sayin, Anti Peg is really unique. She's got jet black hair and she swears a lot. I don' know whether she's got a spot of tha' illness. What that boy on Big Brother had, Two-vets or somethin'.

Anti Peg was Grampa's eldest sister – and apparently was more like a mam to him. There were five of 'em in all. One of them's in Australia now and Gramps is in heaven, but I've never heard the other two mentioned.

I opened the door.

'Aia Anti Peg. 'Ow are ew?'

'Fuckin' hell, let a lady in first will ew? It's pissin' down outside.'

She pushed her way in. She's tiny. She's got a frame the size of a six-year-old. Serious. I don' really understand how she swears so much. I know she used to work with the minin' somewhere. But, I don' think it's nothin' to do with that. I think she just enjoys swearin'. I think she feels younger when she swears.

'Where's ewer Mam then? She better be bastardin' ready.'

'Sorry Peg, she's not goin' to bingo.'

'The little cunt.'

God, that's an awful word. Even if it does make her feel young. I know Mam 'ad said she's on tablets, but bloody hell.

25

'I'll be takin' you instead.'

'Ow, alright. Great. Thank-ew bach. Are ew sure?'

'Yes,' I said, but I didn't mean it. Who in their right mind would want to take two old fogies to the Bingo on a rainy Tuesday night? One of 'em swearin' like a trooper and the other droppin' her bloomers or, worse still, stagin' a disappearin' act. Tomtom came to say hello but Anti Peg just kicked him out the way. He made a cat screamin' noise and farted. Gutted.

As soon as we finally got Nanna out of her bedroom, we were on the bus. Nanna sat on her own in the back and Anti Peg sat with me. For all my sins.

'Ow, it's a cryin' shame to see her like this, she didn't know me earlier on.'

'Aye, she did Peg, she's just bein' stupid. You watch now, when she gets to Bingo. Mam always says she lights up at the sound of two fat ladies.'

'Aye, maybe,' she said.

It must be weird too, seein' someone younger than you gettin' ill in the head. Nanna's loads younger than Peg and she has to watch her gettin' old. I felt really proud of Peg for a moment, fair play to her. She was ancient, and she was really alive.

'Where's Flo tonight Peg?' I asked her. The little dog was always by her side. Usually anyway.

'She's with Nathaniel next door. She bloody hates bingo. Always thinks she's goin' to win, and she sulks for days if she doesn't.'

Peg sat there clutchin' her handbag and lookin' in front of her. Maybe she wasn't as sound of mind as I'd thought earlier. A dog wantin' to win at the bingo? Come on. I looked at her for a bit: she was in another world. All of a sudden, I 'ad this weird feelin' of wantin' to cry. Old women always 'ad their handbags, didn' they. Always. Even if they had nothin' else, they always held their handbags tight.

I turned to look back at Nanna. She was OK. I looked through the windows. The bus was deathly quiet and the Rhondda looked pretty tonight, 'cos you couldn't see it I s'pose. Orange lights and rain, that's all there was. I was about to start relaxin' when Peg started talkin' again. She was seriously knackerin' me out. I just looked at her face while she jabbered on. Her lipstick was all over the shop and she had blue eyeshadow. It was mingin', really mingin'. Then she went quiet again. When we got to the stop, Peg got off before me and I fetched Nanna.

'You alright Nanna?'

'No, I'm missin' *Pobol y Cwm.*'

'Cos we're goin' to the Bingo, mun.'

Nanna turned her head and had a good look at me. I don't think she's ever really looked at me before. I was about to say somethin' when I heard the bus driver shout:

'Get off the bus, you dirty cow! Ewer sick eware!' and all I saw was Peg shufflin' off the bus, laughin'. Cacklin' nearly. I ran down to the front of the bus to see what was goin' on. As I ran, I slipped hard 'cos the aisle was wet and I collapsed on the floor knockin' my 'ead on one of the barriers you hold on to when the bus goes fast or when you wanna get off on the next stop. Nanna stood where she was but Peg came back on. I was dizzy and I was talkin' funny but I remember askin',

'What did you do to 'im, Peg?'

'No matter now darlin', you're 'urt.'

'Tell me.'

'Only if he wanted some anal.'

I didn't even understand what she said, and as I tried to rack my brain what anal meant I fell into a weird, blurry sleep.

When I woke up, I was back on the sofa in the house. I was really gutted too 'cos I had really wanted to see Nanna wake up in Bingo. I tried to ask Mam somethin' but she just patted my hand and said:

'Wha's anal, Mam? Wha's anal?'

'Shush now, you're no' makin' any sense love. You go' concussion.' I heard her mutterin' under her breath, ''cos of tha' nymph aunty of yours. That's where *he* gets if from.'

I felt sick lyin' there, and I didn' want Peg to be blamed for nothin'. Mam needed to understand that these things were followin' me around, regardless of Peg's or anyone's behaviour.

Random Death number three was a lucky escape then. But more than that, it shook me up a bit. 'How did she go then? Poor love'. 'She was runnin' after her 80-year-old aunty who was tryin' it on with a bus driver. Yeah, Sam slipped and hit her head.' 'Oh, and in a bus too, in a bus.' Anti Peg didn't come to visit me the week I was on the sofa. Maggie did mind. All red eyed and sniffin'. She came to see me to tell me that in the last few days she'd been bleedin'. She'd lost the baby. But I knew that wasn't what 'ad happened and I knew there was more to the story. 'Cos I am slightly psychic after all.

Chapter 4

Isn't it funny how things can suddenly change? I don't know what did it either, but the last few days have just put everythin' on a skew. Nanna is playin' up big style. But Mam was the shocker. I haven't long been back in work and she throws a bomb and expects me to deal with the mess. She told me first when I was sittin' on the toilet. She was pluckin' a few hairs from her chin by the mirror when she just blurted out, just like Anti Peg would do,

'I' gorra boyfriend now love,'

'You gorra wha'?'

'A boyfriend.'

'What d'you wan'? A chocolate watch or what?'

'I'm not braggin' Sam, only sayin'.'

'Wha's a woman ewer age doin' avin' boyfriends? You're old enough to be a gran.'

She really went mad. 'Watch your tongue, young lady. Children like you would be drowned in the olden days.'

'Only I'm not a child.'

'Yes you fuckin' are. Any how, I've gorra boyfriend.'

I didn't say a thing so she had to:

'And he's comin' round in a few days' time, for a meal. What d'you think?'

I didn't reply, I knew she'd want me too. She tries to be my friend sometimes, like all pally-pally.

'Aren' ew gonna ask where we met?'

'No. I'm 'avin' a pee, Mam. Couldn' you have waited until I'm decent?'

She just ignored me and carried on. I don' think she's got anyone else to tell.

'In the Legion, the night you got concussed. I went out when you started sleepin'. Funny ol' night too.'

Too fuckin' right, I thought. If I'm honest, the only thing I could think about from that moment on was me. Selfish innit? I always have felt that half me is Mum an' the other half is Dad. 'Course, that's bloody blatant but while Mam wasn't movin' on, I just, well, I just thought there was a chance, I suppose. When Dad comes out like.

'Ewer nor angry are ew?'

'Me? Angry? 'Bout wha'?' I know that winded 'er up. More than me swearin'. She knelt really close towards me, I could actually smell her breath. It wasn't 'orrible, but I could smell it. And worse still, I was on the toilet. With my legs apart.

'You gorra bloody grow up and stop day dreamin' some day, good girl. Dad and me, never again. It never worked. You gorra accept it love.'

She turned more sensitive all of a sudden and tha' made me more mad. But instead, 'cos she was bein' sweet, I just cried. And I never cry. Cryin' is a waste of time. But I did, on the toilet.

'O love. I didn't know how to tell you. I didn't think you'd care so much.'

'I don't,' I said, dribblin'.

'Tell ew wha', you get a nice boy from Custards now and we'll all go out for a meal – and we'll have them pay for everythin'.'

Fuck, things like this really piss me off. Just because she's had months to work things out in her head, and a few days to settle with the idea of 'avin' a new boyfriend, that doesn't mean that I can just take it in just like that. People are like that. Once they've gotten used to an idea, they think everyone else should too. Wendy Moses up the street left her husband and her kids to live with a Pakistani man who owns a takeaway in Porth. Fair enough I know, but two weeks after she did it, she came back to the house with her new man, so that her ex-husband and him could meet. Of course, she had seen this comin' years before, but her ex hadn't. He went mental and trashed the take away. Sprayed all foust racist comments all over the window. Only, he didn't really mean those. What he wanted to write on the window was. 'Wendy, you fuckin' whore.'

'But, whar about Nanna?' I asked her, tryin' to think of any excuse to try and get things back to normal.

'Well, she can come out for food too, if you really want.'

'For fuck's sakes,' I said gaspin' for breath, 'I don' mean tha'. I mean, what about Nanna? How come she's stayin' with us if Dad's never gonna be able to come 'ome? She's Dad's, not ours.'

I got up, it was really squashed in the toilet now. I pulled my knickers up without her seein'.

'O love, did ew seriously think that while Nanna was 'ere there was a chance for . . .'

'No. I know he was a prick.'

'He's not a prick, love.'

'Why did ew always call him tha' then, to his face and to Marian and Beagles on the phone?'

She smiled ''Cos that's what girl friends say about their men.'

'Then why can't ew go back with 'im? If he's not a prick.'

'Well, see, ewer dad is not a prick but he was a prick to me.'

I was so confused by now that I had stopped cryin'. I just

kept lookin' at her. And she kept lookin' at me. Both of us sayin' nothin'.

'Come down stairs! Telly, telly.' It was Nanna. Cradlin' Tomtom in one arm and tryin' to pull my arm with the other. 'Come downstairs.'

I decided that anythin' was better than standin' in the bathroom with someone tellin' me my father was a prick. Surely that meant that half of me was a prick too.

'I'm comin, mun; look, I'm comin' aren' I?'

When we got to the TV room, *Wedi 7* was on again. I looked at the screen long and 'ard. Why had she dragged me down to see that Angharad Mair bird? I turned to Nanna – and there he was on the sofa. Sittin' there next to her, with a suitcase by his side, was the prick.

'How's my little poppet then?'

'Ewer out?'

'Good behaviour.'

'Ewer 'ere?'

'Aye.'

'Does Mam know?'

'No.'

'She's upstairs; go and say hello.'

'No, I don' think I can. Go and tell 'er I'm 'ere. An' I'll text Gareth to tell 'im. He'll be chuffed.'

I smiled at 'im. I love him don't I, 'cos he's my Dad. He never did anythin' to hurt me. He never did anythin' to hurt no one. He just claimed and worked. And did too much bettin'. Didn't hurt no one. 'Cept Mam, that one time. Things changed after that. But that was nothin' to do with him goin' down. I ran from the room, excited and scared. I nearly tripped over Tomtom, who was on the floor by now, all confused with the new smells. I ran like a gallopin' horse upstairs, even though I knew Mam wouldn't want to see 'im. 'Specially after breakin' that news to me earlier on.

Mam was lyin' on her double bed. Mam and Dad's double bed.

'Wha's up bach? Nanna bein' silly again?'

'Aye, she is a bit. Listen Mam . . .'

'Yes love?'

I was about to tell her that my Dad was down stairs, 'er 'usband, he was out, everythin' could be the same, but I couldn't.

'Yes darlin?'

'I'll make us supper tonight, OK?'

She smiled and closed her eyes.

'That's really sweet of you love.'

She opened them again and looked at me, like as if she was proud of 'ow I 'ad taken the news. Truth was I couldn't even begin' to think how I felt about that.

'So stay upstairs while I set the table and do some special surprises yeah?'

''Course.'

I was about to leave her and Dad's room when she shouted.

'Hey,' I looked over and a waft of Mam smells flew over to me and up my nose. Half of me was 'avin' a lie down on a bed while the other half of me was down stairs wantin' to change everythin' back to how it was. 'Thank-ew bach.'

In that strange, weird twenty minutes I think I grew up more than I ever had before. 'Cos I'd lied. Lyin' is a sign of gettin' old, I reckon. I felt sick and dizzy as I told Dad that Mam had a migraine and tha' she wants him to stay at Anti Peg's. Dad didn't look surprised really, just a bit miffed I suppose.

I took 'im to the door and he said that Gareth had texted him back sayin' 'wicked'. And he said that Gareth 'ad been phonin' 'im quite a lot in prison. That made me feel like shit, 'cos I hadn't been phonin' at all. Dad wasn't a bad man. He'd just had it rough durin' the last few years. I smiled at 'im. He wasn't bad lookin'. His eyes were big and wet and he still had a lot of his own hair. That was good, I thought. He could get someone else, maybe, some day. I looked at his nose, and for some reason it reminded me of when I was little. I looked up at him and said, 'Ta-ra'. He held my hand and turned my wrists around.

'Ewer not doin' that shit anymore are you?'

I blushed. I only cut myself for two years. I was over that now. I pulled my hands away. The old scars proved that I wasn't doin' it. I tried not to look at my scars, because it tempted me to slash again. It felt lush, when I did it. But I pushed it to the back of my mind.

'Good. I'm glad.' He smiled, lookin' at the wall. So I looked over as well, and saw a small stain. That was Gareth's. Mingin'. There were bits of us all over the 'ouse. Like memories, I suppose. Dad was on the wall too, 'cos he was the one that put the pictures of American film stars up on the wall. Marlon Brando was his favourite. He hadn't taken it from the 'ouse, 'cos I knew he thought he'd be comin' back. I knew Mam knew that too. He turned and left after givin' me a hug. I felt lovely after that hug. I shut the door and went to the kitchen.

Just like I promised, I started to get things ready for tea. Just when things were startin' to boil over and spit in fat, I heard the doorbell go. Shit, I thought. And I'd just shoved a huge fish finger in my mouth! Shit, I thought, he's back. The prick, my Dad. I ran do the door quick so that Mam wouldn't get the chance to open it. I tried to chew on the fish finger. Standin' there with a smile on his face was this boy.

'Do you wanna buy one of these?'

Bloody catalogues. I 'ad to say somethin' now, didn't I? I pushed the fish finger with my tongue and rested it inside my left cheek.

'No, not really. Thanks tho'.' He must've been about my age, a bit older then. Nineteen, I'd say. He 'ad somethin' about him. And for me to say that, he must 'ave 'ad somethin' about 'im. Green, nearly scary eyes, and rosy cheeks. People in the street think I'm a lezza, I think, 'cos I don't shag about. It's not that I'm a lezza, it's just I don't really fancy a lot of people.

'Oh come on, a pretty girl like you? Don't you wanna buy somethin' for your mum and dad's weddin' anniversary or for your partner?'

Wrong answer, mate. I slammed the door shut and as I did that, the piece of fish finger slid from my cheek to the back of my throat. I 'ad to think quick, I couldn't breathe nearly. I was chokin'. I thought, shit, Nanna won't be able to save me, she's an invalid, or selfish at least and never catches a drift until it's too late. I was chokin', it wasn' movin'. Shit. By the time Mam would come down to 'elp, I would have been with the fishes. I 'ad no choice. I opened the door as the boy with the catalogue was about to get out of sight.

'Awcwww!' I shouted, seriously feelin' like shit by now. He slowly turned around and saw my face. Apparently, I was purple, he said after. I think he was bein' a wanker. 'Please!' I tried to be polite in the face of death. Fair play to me.

He realised what was goin' on, at last, and he ran like the clappers towards me. He whacked and whacked my back. Nothin' appened. I was panickin' now. Sweatin'. Knowin' I was goin' to see Grampa. Then the boy with the green eyes did that thing that Robin Williams does to Piers Brosnan in *Mrs Doubtfire*. Grabbed me with his arms from behind, put 'em around me (but not in a romantic way) and heaved up, heaved up. He did it a few times, but I knew that I was goin' to die. Die of embarrassment too.

'One, two and . . .' out it came like a little gold fish jumpin' from a bowl. The fish finger landin' on our concrete pavement. 'You really ought to be more careful what you put in your mouth before openin' doors to strangers,' he said while I gasped for breath on the ground.

'I thought it was goin' to be my Dad. But thanks, anyway.'

'No worries', he said. 'That'll teach you not to buy somethin' from a poor boy sellin' catalogue merchandise.' He started to walk away and I stood up. I wanted to know his name. I couldn't be arsed to be subtle, so I asked.

'What's your name?'

'Ah, that would be tellin', he said, and away he went. Cocky bastard.

'I'll call you Tellin then,' I shouted after him. That's the Welsh word for harp, that is. I bet he didn't know that.

I ran upstairs again, all knackered and emotional after everythin'. I told Mam tea would be ready soon. As I said it, tears of tiredness came to my eyes.

'Why are you cryin' love?'

'I'm not, I just nearly choked tha's all, gettin' the door.' I didn't think: 'I thought it was Dad.'

Mam sat there stunned. She looked at me all dewy-eyed. I hate it when she gets like this.

'You really expect 'im to be at the door everytime the bell rings?' She started to sob and called me over. 'O come 'ere for a cwtsh darlin'. You expect 'im everyday, don't ew?'

I didn't 'ave the heart to tell her – no actually, I don't expect him everyday. What do you think I am? A simp? He was here, you dosy cow! He was actually fuckin' here, you twat! Here! Today! But I didn't say, I didn't say a thing.

That night in bed everythin' was swimmin' about in my 'ead. I couldn't make sense of anythin'. That Tellin guy to start, and Dad bein' here, him listenin' to me and then leavin', Mam havin' a boyfriend, me and the fish finger. If Random Death number four wasn't enough, surely I'd experienced the most random way ever of findin' someone you fancy. 'How did she go love? Oh, no, a fish finger? Really? Undignified innit? How did they meet, love? Lovely couple they make. How did they meet? Duw, Duw – fish finger. Duw Duw. Wonders never cease!' I fell asleep thinkin' some pleasant thoughts at last. And what were those thoughts? Ah, now that would be Tellin.

Chapter 5

When I woke up this mornin', the stain on the wall by the front door was in my head. Gareth's stain. Weird. It 'ad been there since we were really little. It happened when Mam and Dad went to Brighton on holiday, and Nanna and Grampa came to look after us. Gareth wasn't happy at all, so when Nanna tried to stop him playin' on his gameboy, he went ape. Totally ape. He chucked a chair at the telly, and he was only eight. Then he took Mam's shampoo from the toilet and threw it down the stairs. It was shampoo with colour in it and it dribbled down the wall like tomato sauce. Nanna struggled to get it off while Gramps carried Gareth to his bedroom. He tried to put 'im in his pyjamas but he bit Gramps.

'You should've kept control of him,' Nanna shouted.

'You fuckin' try and keep control of a wild animal.'

I remember runnin' to the kitchen scared and goin' to get a valium for Gareth. Dad used to take 'em when him and Mam argued. And when he 'ad to go on long journeys, because he hated travellin'. I took Gramp one and said,

'For Gar'.

Grampa swallowed it whole and said

'Thank you, love.'

By the end of the night Nanna had sorted everythin' out. She made us all Horlicks and filled half Gareth's mug with whiskey. But the stain is still there today. And Gareth is still majorly embarrassed about that night. Because, usually, he's so normal. Sweet, even.

Anyway, I put the stain and all the other shit to one side, got up and went to Custards. I'm quite 'appy in work still like, but today I 'onestly nearly quit. Somethin' just pushed

38

me over the edge. I was sittin' there sharin' a packet of Quavers with Maggie, when Chief came in. Maggie went all funny and wouldn't look at 'im, and he asked me to come to his office. I stood up and walked behind him. Bloody Nora, he's really tall. He asked me to sit in one of the comfy chairs the other side of the desk. Behind him on the wall, there were two posters of naked women and another poster advertisin' a The Death of the Sales, Man! gig. All the band looked ugly and old. At least twenty-five. Some of 'em nearly thirty. Sweaty and muntin'.

I looked at the naked girls again. One didn't 'ave no fluff on her fanny. And I thought, that's just sick. No, actually it's mingin'. She wasn't even pretty, the girl with no hair, she was 'angin' actually. And hangin' on his wall for everyone to see too. Isn' he ashamed? I thought. Whar if his mother or someone was to come in for some reason and see the naked girl with no hair, and the other with tits the size of those green melons you see in Tesco's? The ones you'd never buy 'cos they're so big, you couldn't ever finish the bloody thing if you tried. It would go all mouldy in the back of the fridge (if it would fit in the fridge in the first place). I tried not to look at the two ladies, who were placed either side of Chief's head. They didn't look like real women. I mean, I'm not fat or skinny-skinny, but I don' look like that naked. I don' think no one does, really.

Chief was quite good lookin', I suppose, some would say. But he 'ad a funny mouth. Always looked as if he was gonna spew. His lips pokin' out a bit too much. Anyway, I decided to get my defence in first:

'I never did nothin'.'

'I never said you did nothin', did I! Why you on the defensive, eh?'

I didn't know actually. I suppose its 'cos you never actually get pulled into the boss's office unless you've done somethin' wrong. They're hardly gonna ask you if you want more pay are they?

'I don' know.'

'Well, then.'

Things went quiet again while Chief fiddled with some paper. The two ladies on the wall, who I decided to call Cassie and Kasey, were all I could look at once again. As if I could do what Chief had done, and put some naked men on my wall. Not that I would ever want to, but as if I could, even if I wanted to.

'I wanna ask for your help and I gotta tell you some things.' Chief looked awkward, not like his usual self.

'With another custard department, is it?' I really didn't want to move, I really didn't. I felt really angry inside, like how I used to feel when the swots always got the questions right before everybody else in school.

'No, I'm not gonna move you.' He went quiet again.

'So? What do you want with me then?' He looked really awkward. He was gonna sack me, I knew it. 'Ewer gonna sack me inew?'

'No, I'm not. It's not about you, it's about someone else,' he said really quick and he put his 'ead in his 'ands. I felt really awkward now. Chief is at least 33. No, tell a lie, he's 32. The eldest in Death of the Sales, Man! When I started workin' in Custards, he had just 'ad a massive party to celebrate his 30th. His mother 'ad come in a wheelchair or somethin' 'cos she 'ad cancer, and she died in the car on the way back from the party. I 'member Gina from accounts blabbin' about it. Gave me nightmares that, too. Mingin' way to go. Not a Random Death at all really, just sick.

40

Anyway, by now I was well confused.

'Sorry, I don' understand. If you don' wanna talk to me, why don' you get the person you need to speak to?'

He looked at me funny and said.

'Don' you understand? It's me, I'm the boyfriend. I was the boyfriend that . . . Don' tell anyone right? If you do I'll be sent packin', cert.'

Oh my God, I couldn't believe it. I was sittin' next to Mam's new boyfriend, I wanted to spew my guts out. He was the one who had told Mam that Dad was no good. He had told her to forget 'im. To forget half of me. He was younger than her too, a lot younger.

'You dirty bastard. Why couldn't she have told me?'

'I thought she had, a few weeks back?'

'Yes, she told me she 'ad a boyfriend. But she never told me it was you.'

'Sorry. I thought she would 'ave, bein' as you see her so much. You look close.'

'How do you fuckin' know? You shouldn't know if we're close or not. It's none of your fuckin' business. You know wha', you've ruined a family. A whole family.' I felt awful sayin' that although I wanted his guts for gutters. I wanted to rip Cassie and Kasey off the wall too. Their tits, out in the open like that, made it all the worse. Thinkin' of Mam with a man with dirty posters on his wall made me wanna spew. Chief was cryin' by now, his sticky-out lips were stickin' out more than they were before. Foust.

'I know I have, I know I have', he kept on splutterin' those words out. He looked a bit too upset to be honest. Why would he give a monkey's about what Mam and Dad had? Or didn't 'ave, 'cordin' to Mam. He was obviously a lunatic too.

'I'm goin' back to my desk alright? I don' wanna hear another word of ewer shit and I don' wan' you ever to say we 'ad this conversation. I wanna hear 'er sayin' it herself.'

He closed his eyes and cried again as I left. I couldn't believe that Mam wouldn't 'ave said nothin'. I felt a bit 'orrible and weird about the whole thing too, 'cos Chief was so upset. I thought, he must be one of those men who cry a lot. Not like Dad, he didn't do that. He just punched a wall if he was upset. I like men more like tha', than cryin' like babies.

When I got back to the desk Maggie was lookin' all big eyed and interested. She looked a bit under the weather too. What was it with this place today? I 'adn't just seen one magpie this mornin', I'd seen three and saluted them too. Things shouldn't be this bad. Then I remembered, I'd put my trainers on the table to do the laces right. Bad luck. That's what it was. I felt responsible all of a sudden.

'What did he want?'

'Oh nothin',' I said. But I couldn't wait longer. I 'ad to tell her everythin'. I was about to start that translatin' malarkey when I thought, bugger it, I'm gonna tell her. 'Mam's gorra boyfriend, Mag.'

'Never. But wha's tha' to do with Chief? What did Chief want? Was he alright?'

''Course he was. He's the boyfriend.'

Maggie looked really shocked, like I did. She welled up and I did too. 'Why you upset, Mag?'

She looked at me hard. She found it difficult to speak at first and then she said, 'I just feel for ew love. You've been waitin' for ewer Dad to get back and now this.'

She made some excuses about 'avin' to go to the toilet

and ran out. I went in to fetch 'er about twenty minutes after but as I stepped in to the toilet I could just 'ear her cryin' like a twat. Seriously cryin'. The whole thing 'ad brought back all the memories about the bleedin', probably. I felt awful, like shit.

I went to sit down and after a while I went back to fetch her again. Only this time, she wasn't there. She must 'ave gone 'ome. So I went back to my desk. I hated bein' on my desk on my own. I felt really naked, without Maggie there too. She was never off, never ill. In early, workin' late. Really late.

Anyhow, I was workin' 'ard on some translation thinkin' 'orrible thoughts about Mam and Chief doin' it, when Big Ben came in. We call 'im tha' 'cos he's big and his name is Ben. Oh, and he's always late for work. Never understood tha' one. He looked funny sometimes, Ben. He always 'ad little cute holes in his t-shirts. He's one of the dopers. I 'ad joined 'em for a spliff for lunch once but I was like a fart all afternoon after smokin' so I never did it again. Ben works on the machinery in the wet custard section. He should never be stoned and operate that stuff, he could seriously die.

'Alright?'

'Yeah, wha' d'you wan?', I didn't mean it funny. I just wanted to break the ice. He took it funny.

'Fine.'

'Sorry, don' worry. Wha' d'you wan' 'en?'

'There's a union meetin' tonight. You comin'?'

Someone came and asked Maggie all the time to go to these things. Think they never asked me before on 'count of the fact I was too young. See, maybe it was visible thar I had grown up in the past few weeks.

'Dunno, I've not got membership.'

'Don' worry 'bout that. It's gonna be interestin' tonight. Six OK?'

I didn't have no choice, 'OK'

'We all go for a cuppa first alright?'

Fair play, he was bein' kind. I could tell. He 'ad a beard. I could tell through the beard even. A funny one. Like all bumfluff gathered together. It didn't look like a real beard.

To be honest, I kind of wanted to go to the meetin' to avoid goin' 'ome. I was still in shock about Chief and Mam and I just didn't want to go 'ome, ever. I knew I'd be better off stayin' and tryin' to calm down. I knew I was gonna bite Mam's 'ead off, but I wanted to be a little more in control. That's all. Therefore, the union meetin' was supportin' me as a worker tonight. Stoppin' me from killin' my mother.

When it came to cuppa time after work, I didn't really want to go. It seemed a bit clicky. They all knew each other and all that. I took a fountain pen and a piece of paper with me. At least I could look like I knew what it was all about. I love fountain pens. They're really cool things. Classy, like. I remember Elen 'ad a really nice one in school, with her name etched in it. Her Mam could afford that. Mr Planky (that wasn't his real name) always told us to use our fountain pens in Hanes. He was a funny one he was: fancied all the girls and let us speak English in the *gwersi* so that we would fancy him back. We loved that.

I had sweaty palms while I was lookin' through the canteen door. There were only four there. Percy, he's ancient and works on the machines with Big Ben who was sittin' there all eyes. Big Ben looked young next to all the rest. Malcolm was there too. 'Malcometh-the-Day', they call him. He's crazy religious. Nice enough though, ancient like Percy. At least sixty. Malcometh-the-Day goes out to Ponty, Treala' and loads o' places with a sandwich board on 'im sayin' things like 'The Lord Jesus watcheth over your every move'. Sounds bloody scary if 'ew ask me. Nanna believes mind. She gets the blind people's tape through the post with a weekly Welsh-speakin' readin' of the Bible. She's not blind mind. Thievin' that is. Stealin' from the blind. I wonder what God would make of that on 'Dydd y Fam'. She's always on about 'Dydd y Fam'. Mother's Day that is, I think.

The other one sittin' there was Ajeet. He's nice enough, got brilliant English. Uses big words I've never heard of. When I hear 'im say a big word in the canteen or on lunch I try and keep it safe in my 'ead for when I get back to my desk. Sometimes I remember, sometimes I don't. Sometimes I've remembered it wrong and it's not in the dictionary how I remembered it. He's got a turban on his 'ead. I think it's really beautiful actually, 'though I'd never say that. I bet it gets bloody hot in the summer, mind. I thought it was quite funny how Ajeet and Malcometh-the-Day were sittin' side-by-side 'avin' a chat. There was a lesson for all the world there, I think. In a custard factory in the Rhondda.

Everyone kept askin' polite things like this to each other:

'You tired? You look tired.'

'You're knackered? Aren' ew? You look knackered.'

No one spoke to me while we drank tea and coffee. I don't think they were bein' cheeky, I just don't think they knew what they should say to a girl my age. We all went to the little pokey room next to the canteen after a while and sat around a table. The table was wood, like old-times tables. The room was smelly. Like cheese or somethin'. My hands felt dirty 'cos I'd been in work all day. I hate that feelin'. I wanted to freshen up.

'Now we'll begin. Anyone checked the minutes? Who

45

wants to second them for me?' asked Percy with a creaky voice. I looked at my watch and said.

'I will. It's just gone six.' They all sort of laughed, but not too harshly. Big Ben turned towards me and whispered,

'Minutes are the notes from the last meetin', see.'

I felt like a real twat, a pillock. I couldn't help but notice that Big Ben 'ad hair sproutin' from 'is ears and nose and he 'ad little bits of dandruff and dry skin on his forehead. Mingin', I thought. He had a beard but he also 'ad little bits of hair sproutin' on the top of his nose. And he wasn't even that old.

They talked for an hour solid. Said that gettin' young people to come to the meetings was gettin' difficult. Said that they wanted to put in the minutes that they were very glad to see me there. I felt quite proud. They said things after that, I couldn't believe. Things about how bad 'Custards' was treatin' us. One of them noted that they knew I did translatin' for free. How the fuck did they know? And anyhow, it wasn't for free. That was my job. I just chewed on the bottom end of my fountain pen, to make sure I didn't say nothin', They said that health and safety 'ad gone down hill, that one of the new boys – Alf I think 'is name was – couldn't believe his eyes some of the things we had to do in Custards. He 'ad been workin' for some carpet place in Merthyr before he came here and he said standards in Custards were shit. Only, he didn't say shit. I just chewed on my fountain pen. One of the men, I don't remember which one now, started complainin' about the way Chief treated some of the staff. Percy called 'im a 'bully' under his breath. The others tutted. I felt a bit weird, as if they were jippin' my Mum. I knew they weren't, but it felt too close somehow, with them two goin' out now. And worse than all that, it just brought everythin' back. The new boyfriend.

The meetin' was finished by seven and everyone smiled at each other. Ajeet pointed at me and said,

'Goodness, you've had a funny turn haven't you. Someone's beaten you black and blue.' Everyone laughed. I was so confused. Big Ben's head and his hairy nose came towards me again.

'You've got ink all over you love.'

I put my hand to my face. I couldn't feel anythin'. I looked at my hand, and it was all dark blue. It was all over my chops, supposedly. I was so embarrassed.

'Open ewer mouth, love,' said Malcometh-the-Day. I did, and they all gasped.

'You better go 'ome love. Looks like you've swallowed quite a lot,' said Big Ben without a smile.

'I 'ope to God it's not Indian ink. You'll be dead if it is,' said Percy. He saw Ajeet throwin' daggers at 'im with 'is eyes. 'Sorry, Ajeet.'

I got a bit panicky. I could feel the stuff runnin' down my throat. At least, I thought I could. I stood up, apologised and ran from Custards down the road. I decided not to stay for the bus, it would take too long. I ran and ran until I reached 'ome. I ran to the sink in the kitchen and washed all the blue shit off me. I gargled, for ages. Blue came out for yonks. I was huffin' and puffin' after runnin' too. I gargled again. Mam and Nanna hadn't heard me come in. They must've been eatin' tea in front of *Wedi 7*. Although, *Wedi 7* must 'ave finished by now. I felt really sick and I was worried that I had ink poisonin'. Shit, I thought. Shit. The only thing that went through my mind was me lyin' in an open coffin and everyone comin' to say goodbye and me with blue all over my chops. Lookin' like hell. Worst of all, I could imagine Chief and Mam comin' up after everyone, holdin' hands. My belly turned. And another thing, they wouldn't be able to give my parts away either, 'cos they'd all be contaminated. Blue, and ugly.

After I'd washed and spat blue for five minutes I went to see Mam and Nanna. I don' think I had been poisoned after all. Nanna wasn't in the front room. But Mam was, with a man. The man was quite stocky, definitely smoked forty a day. I was confused. His face was all red but he 'ad a good nose. Mam just stared at me, so I blurted, 'Gorra telly on my 'ead or wha'?'

'What time do you call this? And what 'ave ew done to yourself? You've got blue all over ewer . . .'

'Alright?' I said to the man next to her. Who the hell was this now? He didn't look like anyone in the family. Not even distantly related. Mam started barkin' again,

'We've been sat here for ages mun. We were gonna take you down the Legion for a bar meal.'

I didn't click, 'Where's Nanna to?'

'In her bedroom. Not feelin' well, that's what she said.'

I didn't understand. The man just squirmed.

'Who's this then?'

'This is Terry love, my boyfriend. Isn't it obvious?' Mam flashed a smile at Terry and he lowered 'is head.

'But wharabout Chief then?'

'Who?'

'O, you've forgotten about 'im then 'ave you? You've made a fool out of me in work and now you've forgotten everythin' 'ave you? You're actin' like a right slag, Mam.'

I felt bad, you should never speak like that in front of strangers. Only in front of family.

'Don't you use language like that in this 'ouse, young lady! The only Chief I know is that Chief who works with you! And I don't even know what *he* looks like.'

48

I was angry. Confused. I wanted to run from the room. I felt like a complete and utter mong. But I was still angry. I turned to the man, Terry, and said.

'Just a warnin' right. She'll probably call you a prick after a while.'

I ran from the room before Mam got a chance to get hold of me, but I could hear her shoutin' my name and cussin' loudly while *Pobl y Cwm* music came on loud. Then someone switched it off. No one understood it anyway. Only Nanna, sometimes.

On the way to my room I popped my 'ead in to see Nanna. She was lyin' on the bed with her eyes open and with Radio 2 blarin'. The curtains were open and she looked hurt.

'Nanna, d'you wan' me to close the curtains for you?' And she just said,

'Broken.' They weren't broken but I wasn't goin' to argue with her. I closed the door and went to my room. I was lyin' on my bed, lookin' at my blue fingers, thinkin'. Why would Chief be such a twat and play such a weird joke on me? What was he talkin' about? Or then, why would Mam not admit to goin' out with Chief? I nearly swallowed my tongue. I nearly wanted to. Shit. Maggie, shit. Cryin' after I told her that Chief and Mam were . . . Shit, shit. I am the boyfriend. Shit. Chief. Chief. Maggie and him. They were shaggin'. Maggie was carryin' his . . . I felt so awful. And Chief had trusted me, wanted me to do somethin' and now Maggie thought . . . Oh my God. I had never felt so shit in all of my life. And guilty too. Never felt as guilty as I did that minute. Like all the guilt in the world was sittin' in my stomach, churnin'. Everythin' churnin', until I had to run to the toilet to spew. The spew was blue and there was nothing else' comin' up. Only spit and water. I wanted to text

49

Maggie, but I didn't know how to say it. I was too chicken to phone. I needed to sleep. When I got back to my room there was a message waitin' for me on my phone. Shit, it's her I thought. But it wasn't. It was a new number. The text just said. 'Want to meet after work tomorrow? Got ur number from ur Nan'. Jesus, I thought! Tellin! The boy with the rosy cheeks and green eyes! Until I saw the name 'dad' and a 'x' at the end of the message. I switched my phone off. Too much to think about. I put on my pyjamas and got in between the sheets. I could still taste the metallic tang of the ink on my tongue. For the first time ever, I felt disappointed that one of my Random Deaths hadn't actually managed to kill me.

I couldn't sleep. I felt really low. When I got like this, only sometimes, there was only one thing I could do to calm me down. My friends in school used to think I was a freak. I went and fetched the radio from Nanna's room. She was sleepin' now too so I closed her curtains. They weren't broken. I threw her Welsh blanket over her and went back to my room with the radio and put it on Classic FM. The music just made me forget I was me. I closed my eyes and saw Maggie's red-rimmed eyes starin' back at me. Mam came in to check on me after, and I just pretended I was sleepin'. I was angry with her, but I couldn't even remember why now. She turned off the radio. And then I heard her go to her room quiet, with another pair of footsteps followin'.

Chapter 6

It's been a random old few days. But today started really nice. Tellin came and offered me breakfast in bed. Toast and those croissant thingies Elen's family used to give us in the morning when I stayed up her house for sleepovers. He told me he loved me and then walked me to the bathroom and came into the shower with me . . . I've been doin' a lot of this recently. Imaginin' that I'm doin' things with Tellin. I can see 'im in my head as if he's there. Some people would say I'm psycho but I just think I've got a wicked imagination. But weirdly, I really do think I know him now. Is that a crazy thing to say?

I've also been speakin' a lot o' Welsh the past few days too. I quite enjoy it but it's much more gay than English. So fussy sometimes, I think. First things first, mind. I 'ad to tackle a lot of things before I got to that bit. Mam and all that stuff. Nanna not speakin' to Mam 'cos of that man Terry comin' to the house – and Maggie, of course.

To tell you the truth, I was shittin' myself the morning I 'ad to tell Maggie about the mix-up I'd made. And I'd come to tell Chief, too. When I got to my desk, Maggie was there already. As per usual. I said good mornin' and she smiled back. She looked totally normal. I could see in her eyes that she was tryin' to forget everythin' that had happened the day before. And with me bein' half psychic and all, it was like the tension was ringin' like an alarm bell in my 'ead. Get stuck in, I thought. Just do it.

'Listen, Mag, about yesterday yeah . . .'

'Yeah, I'm really sorry about tha'. It just . . .'

'Brought some things back. Yeah, I know.'

'Yeah', she said. She wouldn't look me in the eyes. That bugged me more than anythin', and she knew that.

'Anyway', I said, clearin' my throat, 'I got things a bit mixed up, right.' She looked up, and looked like she was blamin' me for everythin' that had ever happened. 'Chief wasn't sayin' that he was Mam's boyfriend, like I thought he'd said.' I lowered my voice to make sure that no one else heard. 'He was sayin' he's yours. I mixed things up. You know how I am.'

Maggie couldn't help but cry but she smiled too, while blubberin'. She looked confused too though, not totally convinced yet.

'Don't cry. It's my fault. He wanted to talk to me about you, I think he did anyway, but I fucked it up. Got it wrong. I've gorra lot on my mind you know.'

Maggie dried her nose on her shirtsleeve, without even noticing she had done it.

'Don't worry biwt, don't worry, right? I know it's not ewer fault,' she sniffled, 'I'm glad mind. I'm fuckin' glad.'

I knew I shouldn't ask anything else, but I was so relieved that everythin' was nearly sorted.

'So, you are goin' out are ew?'

'I didn't think we were after, you know, after the . . .', she didn't need to say it.

'Oh, right. I see. Shall I go see 'im again then? See what he wanted?'

Maggie closed up like a fan again. Scared she was, I think. Scared of what he really wanted to say. Her nose was red and bigger than it usually is, after cryin'. She didn't answer me but I knew I 'ad to go and see Chief. I left the desk without sayin' a thing.

Knockin' on the door, I remembered that I would 'ave to

see Cassie and Kasey again. 'Come in,' Chief shouted and in I went. When he saw me, he turned to stone.

'What do *you* want?'

'I've come to say sorry. I made a mistake yesterday.'

''Bout what?'

''Bout what you said. I thought you said you were my Mam's new boyfriend.'

He looked at me funny, turned his head like a dog.

'Come in then,' he said and as I closed the door, he said, 'Ewer a bit weird you are, aren' you?'

'Wrong end of the stick, that's all.'

'Wrong stick, love.' I couldn't 'elp but smile.

Then there was that funny silence thing again. He looked about the place, like he was lost and I noticed that Cassie was still on the wall but that Kasey, the lady with no hair, had gone. I wanted to ask, more than anythin' in the world, where she had gone. The stupid band poster was still on the wall mind. Cringe!

'So,' he said, all awkward.

'Aye, so that's what I came to say. I understand now, you were talkin' about you, you and Maggie.'

He looked at me as if he was jealous that I could just be honest about them two. Just frank like that. Chief and Maggie. Maggie and Chief.

'Things are complicated right, you'd never understand.'

'Try me,' I thought I was in a film.

'You wouldn't right, ewer a child. You 'aven't got a clue'

'I'm eighteen, and if I 'aven't got a clue, right, how come you called me in yesterday? Must be pretty damn desperate.'

He looked at me for ages. I felt a bit uncomfortable. Then he smirked.

'Aye, you are a funny one. Bloody hell.'

53

'So?'

He held his hands together.

'I wanted to ask you if she'd talked about me . . . or talked about . . . But then, it's obvious, she hadn't had she.'

'Why do you think that? 'Cos she never said your name?'

'Dunno.'

I couldn't be bothered to play games. How come I was bein' dragged into another relationship problem? It was bad enough me bein' in the middle with Mam and Dad.

'Look, I'm not gonna bullshit, right. If you would 'ave asked me yesterday how she felt, and I would've understood the first time what you meant, then I would've said forget it. For-get-it. But after the way she was when she thought you were bonkin' my Mum . . .' He made a funny face. Sod.

'After the way she was what?' Men piss me off. They wanna hear all the gory details about how much a woman loves 'em. It's absolutely pathetic. Massagin' their egos and their cocks at the same time.

'She was upset yeah? She looked like she, like she . . . likes ew.' I stood up. I couldn't take much more of this bullshit. I looked at him and he said,

'Thank you.'

I just said, 'Don't thank me, sort things out. She's been through hell and back.'

I felt a bit funny bein' so bossy to someone high up in work. But he'd asked for it. See, really, I wanted to say 'Don't thank me, sunshine', but I thought I might be pushin' my luck if I said that. When I left, I noticed that I'd said the sayin' wrong. It was, to hell and back, not through hell and back. Shit.

Anyhow, as far as I was concerned, I 'ad removed myself from that situation. I was glad of it too. Maggie asked some

questions when I came back to the desk but I just said nothin'
and explained that Chief wanted to speak to her sometime.
After lunch, there was a little post-it note on my desk. It was
pink, pretty. It was a note from Chief sayin' – 'Girl from
Welsh Language Commission comin' in at 2.30 to see you.
Cheers for earlier.' I crumpled it up. What he'd written
looked as if I 'ad given him a blowjob or somethin'. 'Course,
I 'ad to uncrumple it 'cos I didn't remember who was comin'
to see me or when. It's an arse of a thing when you 'ave to do
that. No one came to see me usually so this was weird.

But someone came today. And when she came, I could
smell her up the corridor before I met her. The perfume she
was wearin' was lush and, when I saw her, I think my jaw
dropped. She was stunnin'. I was in black trousers and trainers
and my work top and she was in a tiny little purple suit. She
smiled really nice. Her hair was tied so tight in a ponytail that
it dragged her eyes to either side of her face. Pretty mind. All
the men stopped workin' in my side of the buildin'. They
didn't wolf whistle or nothin', but they did stare. They
wouldn't dare wolf-whistle. I felt lucky, that I was the one she
had chosen, or someone had chosen. 'Course, she was gonna
speak Welsh, but I didn't mind much. That was nothin' for all
the excitement she brought. Chief led us into a little room and
sat down with us.

'As the line manager, I should sit in with you really.'
Line-manager? Right, whatever, I thought. You just wanna
look at her tits.

'Ok, great. Well, thank you . . .?' asking for his name with
her eyes.

'Martin. Martin Grisham.' He looked at me quickly.
Bloody Nora, I thought. Martin Grisham!

'A ti?' she asked me with a smile.

55

'Fi yw Samantha, miss.' Oh my GOD! How embarrassin? She ignored the whole thing and carried on smilin'. I liked her before but I liked her even more from then on.

'Dwynwen dw i.' And Dwynwen spoke half in Welsh and half in English. She was on anther planet, mind: the things she thinks we'll be able to do in Welsh. She wants me answerin' the phone in Welsh and all. My arse. The thing that bugged me was that Martin was noddin' back and forth, pretendin' to understand the Welsh bits. It is awkward, mind, when people can't speak Welsh in a room with people who can. When she spoke to me in Welsh, I felt like it was our little secret. Funny innit? I s'pose it was in a way.

Anyway, the meetin' finished much too quick. She nominated me the Welsh Language Officer of Custards, which I think is well funny, considerin' I had a C in literature and a D in language GCSE. Anyhow, I didn't complain. She gave me these pins to give out to people who can understand or speak Welsh in work. Like a badge it is. The bad thing was that I knew no one in Custards would wear one and that they would be at the bottom of the drawer by the end of the day.

I said, 'Mae dim lot o pobl siarad Cymraeg yn Custards.'

She said I'd be surprised how many people could speak Welsh, and Chief agreed. What the fuck does he know anyway? She said that if I was translatin' I should go on a course to make sure my Welsh was spot on. I was gettin' a bit scared. I'm only translatin' for a little while, that's what I told her. I'm not sayin' I'm perfect. But it doesn't need to be perfect does it? She looked at me quite angry and said that it had to be perfect or else the company would 'ave to pay for it to be done. I smiled, I agreed, she smiled back. And she meant it. She liked me, but I don't know why. I wanted to write Welsh perfect but how did I know if I was right? Ever?

She stood ready to leave and shook both of our hands. She smiled again and said to me,

'Ti'n gwbod, os oes gen ti awydd gwella dy Gymraeg, mae angen i ti siarad mwy. Oes rhywun yn siarad Cymraeg lle ti'n byw?'

Yes, there was one family who spoke Welsh on the street. But they were poshos. How come Dwynwen didn't live on my street? And yes, she was right, I needed to practise my Welsh more now. From now on, I was gonna try a bit. Only a bit – with Nanna maybe. And I might, might go and see the poshos. Dwynwen left the room, everyone in our side of the factory stopped as she swished passed. Her lovely smell and her purple suit disappeared round the corner and she was gone.

*   *   *

I went that night, with Dwynwen in my 'ead, to the Welshies' house up the street. They are so rich that the husband built the house on a patch of green by my estate. It's huge and the name on the gate is 'Cartref'. Home. Which is a bit obvious if ew ask me. And a bit gay too. Anyway, I was about to ring the doorbell when I got the jitters. What would I ask? I looked like a right plonker. Meryl, the mam opened the door. I said why I'd come. Wanted to make my Welsh better. She looked shell-shocked and pleased. She looked knackered too.

'Wel, tyd fewn. 'Di Gwenllian na Gareth ddim yma heno cofia.' The kids were not home. Shit. Gwenllian 'ad 'er 'arp lesson and Gareth was training with Ponty Under 21s, apparently. Our Gareth's in Iraq, I wanted to say. But that wouldn't 'ave 'elped, would it? Gwenllian was my age, she was in six form. She was alright with me in school, we talked

57

on the bus. In English. But then, you just drift don' you? In Ysgol Gynradd we did do runnin' and things together. I could speak Welsh just like her then. Meryl said she didn't see her husband much. He was a contractor. Worked in Cardiff lots, comes back late. All that. Like Dad, I explained, done time. Yes, she said, quite.

She asked me how Mam was. I remember they argued once 'cos we 'ad a dog called Moosh and he attacked their cat. Cringe. I'm sure I went red when I remembered that. Meryl was nice, fair play. Said she was on her way to French lessons. Two languages not enough? She asked me if I wanted to stay and 'ave supper with her, before she went to French. Bean burgers and jacket potatoes. Fuck me, I'd rather eat shit than eat that type of food. I said, thanks but Nanna wanted me back to watch *Pobol Y Cwm*. She smiled and I left, feeling cheap and stupid.

She'd said, call again, but I knew I wouldn't. I'd just tried it, for Dwynwen, goin' to see the people you know who speak Welsh. I had tried but it just didn't work. They were somewhere else to where I was. It started rainin' buckets while I was walkin' back to the house, but I didn't run. I just kept on walkin'. And I cried a bit too. What the fuck was wrong with me? Was it Mam and Terry, or Maggie? I don't know.

When I got back to the house, Nanna was already watchin' *Pobol Y Cwm*. I walked in all wet. Drippin'. She smiled when I came in. Glad of the company, probably. I tried some Welsh with her and she laughed. Probably 'cos she couldn't believe her ears. Tomtom was sittin' in her lap, purrin' and he turned his head too. I tried again and she answered, pointin' to the telly,

'Tro fe lan, tro fe lan!', she wanted me to turn the volume up. I looked for the remote controls but they were under the sofa or somethin'. That man Terry must 'ave put it somewhere we don't. Idiot. I stood up and went towards the telly. As I pushed the volume knob somethin' fuzzy came over me. I was shakin' like a leaf. I tried to shout 'Nanna!' but I couldn't. I tried again. She noticed what was happenin' – and left the room! My God, I thought, my own Nanna 'as bloody well murdered me. But, that second, I felt the power go out of me and I dropped to the floor like a sack of potatoes. She had gone to the box by the front door and turned off the electricity. Next thing Mam was shoutin' like a banshee from upstairs.

'What the FUCK'S goin' on? The shower's fuckin' well freezin'!'

Nanna ignored her and patted me on the forehead.

'Paid ti becso. Paid ti becso.'

That night on the sofa, with Nanna's Welsh blanket over me, I was so tired. What with the electric shock and all that Welsh speakin'. I thought funny thoughts too. I wondered, after my Random Electric Death, if Nanna would have arranged a proper Welsh funeral for me. Like they have in Caernarfon and all those places. Bara brith and Welsh cakes. Everyone wearin' daffodils on their suits and my Dad singin' 'Calon Lân' at the top of his voice. 'Cos he'd be able to sing, wouldn't he, if he could speak Welsh, or as long as he was rat-arsed anyway.

When I went to bed that night Mam came to tuck me in. She never did that usually. I think she was a bit pissed. She'd been out with Terry in the Legion. Her breath smelled like alcohol and fags, but I quite liked it. She was bein' really nice to me, I think 'cos she knows I've been in the wars recently – and she didn't even know about the electric shock because I didn't tell her.

After a while, I knew there was a reason she was tuckin' me in and smoothin' my arm.

'Duw, this is jus' like what it was like when you was little. And Gareth in the other room.' I smiled and started to close my eyes. I was driftin' when she said, 'Why didn't you tell Mam that Dad was out?' I opened my eyes again. Wide-awake I was now.

'Dunno, didn't think you'd be bothered.'

'Didn't think I'd be bothered?'

'Didn't think you'd want to know. 'Cos of that man Terry.'

'Stop callin' him "that man"!', she said and stood up. 'You know you should've told me love. You can't hide important things like that.'

'I just wanted you to hear at the right time, that's all.'

'The right time for wha'? There'll never be a right time.'

She walked out of the room and said a tired goodnight. I don't think she was angry with me, just stressed out with the whole thing. I checked my phone before I went to sleep and saw that Gareth had texted me. Fuck, I thought, he must've had a bad day. He never texts. He must be missin' home. He just uses me he does. The text said somethin' different to what I expected though. He was thinkin' of me, I think.

'Alright lil sis. I heard Dad's out. Gutted. Don't get too wrkd up. Mam and dad r old nuff to sort it out thmslvs.'

God, I thought, for someone who isn't the least bit psychic, he did quite well. I went to sleep straight, still really, really tired and weak after the 'lectric shock. I dreamed of guns and texts and wars, and Nanna on *Pobol y Cwm*. I woke up sweatin' in the middle of the night. After that, I don't remember a thing.

Chapter 7

I experienced a very Random Death today. It was weird 'cos I'd been dreamin' about Nanna all night. She was smilin' in my dream, really happy 'cos we were in bingo. She swallowed one of the bingo balls and then fell asleep.

When I woke up, the house was quiet. It's always quiet mind, but this quiet was different. I had been goin' to work everyday that week with my old radio walkman on, listenin' to Radio Cymru, the Welsh radio. I was tryin' to keep up with my practice and do what Dwynwen had said. See, I thought if I can't speak to real people in Welsh then I best listen to the radio. When I'm on the bus the news is on, which is alright. But then, when I get halfway to Custards, this weird man comes on. Joan-zee or somethin' his name is. I'm not bein' funny, but he's not my cup of tea. I don't nearly understand 'im (although I do really) and he gets on your tits 'cos he says stupid things like 'Edrych ar fi pan ti'n siarad gyda fi' to people who phone in. 'Look at me when you speak to me!' What's he on? He's on the radio. Well, anyway, I switch it off then. Loads of people on the bus 'ave got those MP3 players. I can't see the point of those really. Radio I'm into, and most of them too, so why spend all that money on a machine that can do things they'll never use? They do look cool, mind, and they're so light. My walkman's heavy, makes me walk funny actually. Depends what pocket I put it in.

Anyhow, that week 'ad been busy, I hadn't been home much. Workin' late, goin' with Arse to Merthyr and we 'ad a union meetin' (where Percy farted and we had to evacuate the room). I know I'm goin' off on a tangent. I guess I don' wanna come to the punchline, do I? Like I said, I woke to this quiet and went downstairs to get some toast. But I didn't call in to say good mornin' to Mam – in case that-man-Terry was there. I wouldn't be able to be arsed to see anythin' like that.

Downstairs, I was the first one up. Mam wasn't workin' early. And Nanna wasn't there. She doesn't get up early when she's been to bingo. That usually shatters her out and you won't see her for dust. But she hadn't been to bingo, so I had a funny feelin'. Don't ask me why. After all, I am a little bit psychic. I went upstairs and knocked on her door. I poked my head in to see. She was lyin' there, in bed. Sleepin'. I went over to see her and she was holdin' her Bible. I got it from her hands, and then I realised her hands were cold. In that order. I sort of looked at her for a while. She looked quite pretty. Well, as pretty as an old woman can look. She was dead, mind, I knew it. I put the Bible on her sideboard and a picture fell out of it, on to the floor. I picked it up and there it was. The picture I had in my head. Both of us dreamin'. Still. Mam and Dad holdin' me. I was tiny. And Gareth playin' about on the floor. She wanted it all to go back to that didn't she? My Nanna.

I didn't tell Mam until she came downstairs. I didn't see the point in wakin' her. In the meantime, I phoned work to tell 'em I'd be late. They said they were sorry to hear. I went upstairs to Nanna's room again and put the Welsh blanket on her. I felt like an idiot. What was the point in tryin' to keep someone dead warm? But then, I knew she would 'ave liked the blanket on her, if she was still alive.

I sat in the kitchen feelin' upset. I didn't cry mind. I was beyond cryin'. I felt awful for Nanna that she had to live to see that-man-Terry turn into the resident man in our house. It didn't seem right somehow. I remembered, too, that mornin'

that she'd talked about that curtain bein' broken the night
before. It wasn't the curtain broken, I knew that. I knew at
the time too. It was her. I just couldn't bring myself to even
think it. When Mam found out, she didn't say much,
although tears ran down her face. Turns out that-man-Terry
wasn't there after all so I could've woken her earlier. But I
was glad I hadn't risked it.

That night came quick and Nanna was in a box in her
room. We'd been really busy with loads of things all day.
Mam phoned Dad to tell him. I felt awful thinkin' it, but I
reckon Dad was upset for losin' Nanna more 'cos of the fact
that he wouldn't know our house anymore. Without her
there, his flesh and blood, he wasn't as much a part of things.
Only half of me was left for him. Weird really, Nanna and
Dad didn't really ever speak. Not recently anyhow. Mam
phoned Anti Peg too. She just said down the phone,

'No fuckin' way. Never. I always thought I'd pop mine
before her.'

She came down for a cuppa tea-time and was a good
laugh, actually. Dad came to fetch her. At one time, me, Mam,
Dad and Anti Peg sat round a table 'avin' a decent
conversation. I was watchin' Mam and Dad really close to see
whether I could see love comin' between 'em again. I enjoyed
seein' 'em sit together. Mam, Dad, next to each other. Sayin'
Mam, Dad, Dad, Mam over and over in my head. But I didn't
see no sparks. Nothin'. Not even an argument. I couldn't help
feelin' that Nanna 'ad died for this meetin' to 'appen. I turned
to look at Anti Peg at one stage; she looked devastated but she
just carried on tryin' to make us all laugh.

By the time *Wedi 7* was on, everyone had gone. Mam had
gone to see Terry – she'd asked me if I minded and I'd said
'No.' I meant it too. I didn't give a shit, bein' in a house with

a dead person. 'Cos it wasn't just any old dead person, it was Nanna. I sat there watchin' *Wedi 7*, feelin' a bit bored actually 'cos they were at this big old-fashioned mansion where that Iolo Williams bloke with massive legs was launchin' a book about walkin'. Then Angharad Mair came on again. She looked really pretty, like what I wanted to look like. She spouted Welsh and made me jealous. I felt like shit. I went to the kitchen, made myself a cuppa and just looked at the new cupboard for a while after that. It must have been for a while 'cos when I went back to sit on the sofa, *Pobol y Cwm* had started. I felt a bit funny when it came on. All sick and sad. That was when I really realised that Nanna was gone. I wouldn't 'ave the chance again to be forced to watch *Pobol y Cwm* and pretend I didn't want to. I watched it anyhow. I watched it for her. And I quite enjoyed it.

After it finished, I felt really flat. For a while when it was on, I'd pretended that she was there watchin' it with me. Is tha' sick? Not tha' we talked when we used to watch it together; she would just fart, real loud. Anyway, after the adverts came on, I had this idea – and I just did it. I went upstairs and into Nanna's room. She was lyin' in the open coffin, but I'll call it a box. It sounds nicer in my head. She 'ad a Welsh blanket on her body and didn't look sad. I sat on the little cream stool by the bed. The stool was really low, and what with the coffin bein' so high up, I couldn't see a thing. But it didn't matter anyway. I sat there, with the lights off and told Nanna the story of what 'ad 'appened on *Pobol y Cwm* that night. I started off sayin' in English and then really slowly I started to change to Welsh. I got stuck sometimes and put some English words in. I thought I would cry for a minute, but after a while I felt loads better 'cos I 'ad a feelin' she was enjoyin'. After I said this line, I left her:

'Bydd fi'n watsho nos fory i chi i gweld beth sy'n ddigwydd, a pob nos.'

I told her I'd watch it tomorrow night for her to see what 'appens. But I knew I'd never tell her again really. Not like this. I cried then, only for a second and then I went out. As I came from the room, I noticed Tomtom was lyin' by Nanna's door. Later on, when I went to bed, he was still there.

When I came downstairs Mam and Terry were sittin' in the lounge. I thought I best make an effort 'cos Mam must 'ave be feelin' sad too so I went in and sat with them. Terry was watchin' a comedy. I didn't think that was very thoughtful. Mam looked as if she was alright, mind. When I came in, Terry reached for the remote controls from the top of the sofa and turned the sound down. So that's where he kept them. Twat. He smiled at me in a nice way and I thought I smiled back, but come to think of it, I don't think I did, 'cos he looked offended. Who gives a shit anyway? He hasn't lost his Nanna this mornin' has he? Mam asked me if I was OK,

'Alright bach? 'Ave Gareth phoned?'

'No.'

'Sure?'

''Course I'm sure. Fuck's sakes, what do you think I am? Deaf?'

'Sorry, love . . .' , Terry butted in, 'Ewer Mam just wants to know he's safe, and whether he's comin' back like. To the funeral.'

I wasn't thick. I knew that's why she was askin'. But then, he didn't know that did he, that I wasn't thick. I said, I know, and I said I better go to bed.

'It's only just gone nine, love.'

'You into sports, Sam?', Terry asked, all keen and irritatin'. This is hardly the time to ask a question like that, I thought.

65

'No', I said, 'sorry.'

'No matter', he said under his breath and I felt sorry for him. But, why should I? If it wasn't for 'im, Dad and Mam would be here together now. Only, I knew really, deep down, that it was fuck all to do with him. I made some excuses and left. I just couldn't handle it. As I went upstairs, I noticed somethin' different about the wall. The picture of Marlon Brando 'ad gone.

The funeral's not 'til next week. They've got to do tests on her 'cos she wasn't that old, supposedly. I thought she was ancient, mind. Everythin' went back to normal after the day Nanna slept for the last time in our house. I missed her misbehavin' mind. Her gettin' lost, me goin' to find her. I offered Anti Peg we go to bingo but she said she never could do bingo again without Gwen. I thought it was funny, it was the first time I'd ever heard anyone call Nanna Gwen. I thought it sounded really weird. And I decided I was gonna call my little girl Gwen, when I'd 'ave one.

Work 'ad given me an extra day off, fair play. So, I phoned Arse to see if she wanted to meet again. Just before Nanna had died we'd had a really good time in Merthyr. Bloody hell, that retail park is deadly. We had a pizza in one place and a knickebockerglory thingy in KFC. All the people sittin' on the tables were gobblin' their food down. A woman on the table next to us was so fat, she needed two seats. No one else was that fat mind, but she was huge. We saw two girls from school too. Charlie (she came from Essex to our school when she was fourteen) and Emma Lloyd. They both 'ad pushchairs. Mind you, eighteen is old enough to be a mam if you ask me. We said hello, but we didn't have much in common really. We hardly spoke in school, so why would we have somethin' to say now? The babies were well cute, mind, especially Emma Lloyd's. Her boyfriend was black and the baby had lush skin and corn rows all over her head. Arse and me went to look in Topshop after, and I bought a necklace for myself. She made me laugh so much, all the way round the shop, until I nearly pissed myself. Literally.

Anyway, when Arse and me met again a while after, things were even better between us. Last time was the first time I'd seen her for a while and it takes a while to oil the wheels, doesn' it? This time she took me down Ponty Park. We walked around for ages, then she started talkin' about her new boyfriend. Alex his name is, works for her step dad. Arse is a pretty girl, like, and I don' mean this funny, but men definitely think she's prettier than women do. She's blonde, quite small, wears a lot of make-up. Underneath that, she's . . . I don' know . . . I wouldn't call her goppin' but she's not stunnin'. I think it's important to be honest about these things. But, boy does she have an arse. Hence her nickname. We were both wearin' big coats today 'cos the clouds were heavy and black. It never rained, mind.

We were leanin' against James James and Evan James, who wrote 'Mae Hen Wlad fy Hadau', when she giggled and said:

'Member in school, when you copped Damian Cooper?'

'Yeah,' I said. God, I didn't even remember that. In the toilets.

'Member how Mrs Cradoc went mad, told you not to sell ewer body . . .?' she laughed again.

'Aye, but she would say that. She's a Christian, an evange . . . you know . . . one of those.'

Arse put her hand to her face. She was so girly. Then she reached into her coat pocket and fetched a fag. Offered one to me. No, I didn't want one, but she looked well cool doin' it mind.

'We were so naïve back then. Think about it. Talkin' about if you'd used tongues and all tha'.' I smiled.

'I know. I got his chewin' gum after that.'

'Are you seein' someone now?' She went in for the kill. And for some reason I said,

'Kind of.'

'No way! Who? Why didn' you tell me? You tit!'

In a way, I felt as if I was goin' out with Tellin. Only, I really wasn't. She dragged on her fag hard and threw her head back. I could see why boys liked her.

'Oh, it's nothin'.'

Arse played with her hair and leant back on Evan .

'Come on now, I wanna know all the gory details. We can share all our experiences now. Has he asked you to . . . you know?' She pointed at her bum.

'No,' I said. Because he hadn't.

'Have you . . . you know . . . gone down . . .'

'No,' I said. Because I hadn't.

'What 'ave you done then?'

'We're takin' things slow.'

'Oh, right,' said Arse straightenin' herself and draggin' on the fag again. 'I shagged Alex on the first night. I couldn't help it. The chemistry was just . . .' She blew the smoke from her lipstick mouth.

I didn't want to know anythin' else. Arse was a cool friend to 'ave, but I didn't want to know the A-Z of her sex life. At least, not without havin' drunk a bottle of vodka first.

'We should really go on the piss some day,' I said, lookin' at Arse with a determined look, tryin' to change the subject.

'Aye, defo. I'll bring Alex, and you can bring . . .' she asked me for his name with her eyes.

'Tellin,' I said, and it felt weird to say it, actually. I felt as

68

if I was goin' out with him. 'Yeah, cool, but I'd love a girly night out first.'

Somethin' flashed to the front of Arse's mind.

'My GOD! I can' believe I haven' told you. Last Friday I was down Cardiff with some of my college friends, yeah? From Health and Beauty . . .'

'Yeah,' I said.

'And I saw Mr Warner, 'member that young supply teacher who was really nice to us. Flirted even. *Chwaraeon* teacher, he was. He had a funny accent.'

'Yeah?' I said.

'And he was standin' with one of the boys from The Bewildered, who played the Full Ponty. It was in a bar on St Mary' St. O'Flanighans yeah? That's where all the rugby boys go and all. People like Mike Phillips. Anyway, I went to say 'Hi', 'cos Mr Warner really fancied me in school, don' you 'member? I don' mean it big-headed like, but he did, didn't he . . .'

'Yes,' I said, because it was true.

'But the bastard pretended he'd never met me before. Nearly ignored me.'

I felt awful for her. It was true, some male teachers in school were really flirty and this twat was the same. But when us girls came to Cardiff or they saw us on their own turf, they didn't want to know. Twat.

'Anyway, I'm over it, but I thought tha' was not on. He blatantly wanted me in school. But I wasn' good enough for 'im out in Cardiff. 'Cos I'm too . . . I don't know . . . too . . . somethin'.' Arse looked hurt, and then she threw her fag to the floor and stamped on it. 'Listen,' she said, 'I gorra go now, I'm havin' a Brazilian done and then I'm pickin' Alex up. But next time I see you, I wanna know all the gory details

69

about you goin' down on . . .' she searched my eyes for his name again.

'Tellin,' I said.

'Aye, Tellin,' she said, smilin'. She winked, gave me a kiss and waddled away. I love her, but fuck, she's a handful.

She turned back after a while and cringed me out: 'We'll 'ave to go down Ann Summers together and all now!'

The next day, I started back in work and everyone was really nice to me. First day back on the bus was weird. I felt as if I 'ad been away for absolutely ages, although it was only two days. On the way, on the bus, we were on Treepow Row I think, but don't quote me, when I saw Tellin. I couldn't believe he was in front of my eyes. I didn't know if I should put my head down or wave at 'im. I didn't get a chance either way, because he waved at me!

Let me explain. The bus 'ad stopped 'cos there were cars comin' the other way and that's when I saw the boy with a bag over his shoulders. He was holdin' a catalogue. I smiled, thinkin' it might be him but knowin' in my hat of hearts that it wouldn't be. But it was. I don't know why he turned round but he did, and his green eyes just jumped out. Full of colour. He was still good lookin'. He saw me quick too, gave me a smile and waved. I wanted to run off the bus and say somethin' but I couldn't. I just smiled a bit and carried on listenin' to Radio Cymru. The news was nearly finishin' and I was ready to turn it off before that man from North Wales came on. The bus started movin' and I turned my head to look at 'im. I knew he would've carried on walkin', but I secretly thought he might've stayed put and stared. I turned round, and he'd gone. I was gutted. But such is life and I can't be arsed to be bothered. In my head, we were goin' out, and I felt quite safe knowin' that. For a moment, he stops the bus, jumps on and runs towards me. Suddenly, the bus turns into this Turkish tent and he's wearin' some kind of Arabian headgear. After that, he feeds me Turkish delight (I love it when the witch did that on *The Lion, the Witch and the Wardrobe*). Then he kisses me and the taste of Turkish Delight pours between our mouths. The whole thing got a bit dirty from then on so I blinked and found myself sittin' next to the same old man who had kept me company from my stop. I feel like I know 'im. Tellin that is, not the old man! I feel like we'll be together forever, although I've only ever talked to him once.

In work Maggie was really chirpy, said she was happy just 'cos life was cool and 'cos I needed cheerin' up. I said I didn't need cheerin' up. Said that the time of bein' sad 'cos your Nanna's died is natural and good for you. I do 'appen to think that but I really wanted to catch her out too. No way was she actin' all 'appy as Larry just 'cos of me. No way.

'Spit it out then.'

'Wha'?', lookin' all innocent.

'You know wha'. You know who! Sorted everythin' out?'

'Suppose,' she said, biting' her lip. I bloody hate it when smitten girls do that. Winds me up a treat.

'Good news. I'm chuffed for you.'

'Thanks.' And that was that. There was still somethin' a little bit sad about her too. 'Cos although she was 'appy there *was* someone missin' from their life now. So in a way, we were both in the same boat, but she never knew that.

I didn't do much translatin' today, work's fizzlin' out. Which I'm glad about on one hand and sad about on the other. Funny, that type of feelin'. On the way back on the bus, I had my fingers crossed I'd see Tellin. I kept lookin' everywhere to see if he was comin' out of people's houses.

71

But he didn't come and I didn't see 'im. I knew I wouldn't see him, but it was fun just lookin'. I know he's thinkin' about me now. He might be plannin' to stand in the same place as this mornin' tomorrow, and we'll wave to each other again and share Turkish Delight.

When I got home Mam went mad (mad happy) and said Gareth was comin' 'ome for the funeral. I said, he could 'ave my room but she said quietly that he was goin' to stay with Dad and Anti Peg. Terry came after that and I just went to my bedroom. I didn't mind really. Anythin's better than sittin' in the lounge with a stranger holdin' your remote controls.

Chapter 8

Arse had let Elen know that Nanna had died, so when I woke a couple of mornins before the funeral there was a really nice text waitin' for me.

'Flin i glywed am dy nain di Samx'.

I was grateful and yet I knew she'd moved on now, to better people. More Welshy people, people with more prospects. She was just bein' sympathetic 'cos she had to. She can't 'ave meant it really.

I lay there with my hair all over the pillow and crusted spit on the side of my lips thinkin': when was the last time I went to a funeral? Actually, it was when Gramps died. Not that long ago really. I was in year nine, and on the same day as he died of lung cancer (he smoked loads), a girl called Brwyn Heledd died in my school. I remember feelin' really weird about that because she was only thirteen and Gramps was old. Quite old anyway. I remember feelin' guilty that I felt more sad for Gramps than Brwyn, because I knew 'im more. Truth is, he'd lived, and Brwyn hadn't. She choked on her spit in the *ffreutur* after havin' a fit. I was out on the field when it happened. I remember the ambulance, I remember the teachers' faces. I also remember the mornin' after when Ms Sian Owen stopped me on the way to *gwasanaeth*. She stopped me in the corridor on this really sad day. She looked as if she could spit at me:

'Ym, Samantha, beth yn union yw'r colur hyll 'na ar dy wyneb di?' Gypin' my make-up first. Then, 'Ac, ai sannau gwyn wyt ti'n eu gwisgo?'

Was I wearin' white socks to school? Had I dared? White fuckin' socks. White fuckin' socks. I remember wantin' to tear her hair out and bite her eyes. Was that really fuckin' important was it? On a day like this? I suppose, lookin' back, she was takin' her emotions about Brwyn Heledd out on me. I know she really liked her. But fuck, I couldn' help feelin', if it was me who had died, she wouldn't have taken things out on Brwyn Heledd. I hope that Ms Owen's happier now. I hope she's grown out of lookin' to see if everyone's wearin' black socks. And I hope she's 'avin' sex, 'cos I reckon deep down that's why she was so petty. Munter.

There was still a few days before the funeral and I couldn't really be bothered to wait no more now. Sometimes it's just time, isn't it? And what's weird too is that Mam was kind of excited for it. 'Cos of Gareth comin' home. There's somethin' sick about someone bein' excited for a funeral to 'appen. I know it's not quite like that, but it is too in some way, isn't it? Alison, Dad's sister is comin' from Bristol to the funeral and Anti Peg is makin' this big fuss about this man called Danny Bishop from down Cardiff way. She's been makin' a real big fuss that she wants 'im to come to the funeral. I got a bit confused after that. I never knew my Grampa really, not really. I mean, he was around for a while but he died then and I wasn't old enough to appreciate him. Not really. Cancer he had. He went quick. I don' think he knew me really. 'Cos when you're fourteen, you 'ardly know yourself, do you? Or maybe you know yourself but adults can't know you. That makes me more sad in a way than losin' Nanna, 'cos at least we 'ad a chance to get to know each other. He was gone before I was me. Anyway, I got to thinkin' then about this Danny Bishop and in the end, the only thing I can think is that Nanna 'ad to marry Grampa 'cos she was pregnant. I dunno mind, I was just thinkin'. And then I got to thinkin', how come Nanna's name was Gwen,

74

all pretty and Welshy Welsh and she called her girl Alison and her son Ryan? That's Dad that is, Ryan. That's his real name. I think that's weird that they're not Welshy names like Nanna's. I don' know exactly where Nanna came from mind. And I'll never bloody know now. 'Cept, Anti Peg will know. I'll ask her the day of the funeral. Or maybe not on the day of the funeral actually.

It was Saturday by the time my head stopped spinnin' and I was doin' my usual sittin' about watchin' telly. I really like nature programmes and documentaries about Hitler and people. The more evil they are the better, really. It's more fun and crazy to watch. Mam 'ad given me a mountain of ironin' to get through as well. I was doin' that when that-man-Terry came in to the lounge,

'You alright?'

'Yeah.'

'Out tonight isit? On the piss?', he asked. None of ewer fuckin' business I thought.

'No,' I said, and that was the truth.

'Wha's wrong with ew, girl? Get out there, mun. You should be rat-arsed every Saturday ewer age. Steamin'!'

'Yeah, and you shouldn't.' I hated that I was bein' like this but I couldn't see what other way to be. He looked at me real funny and shook his head.

'I dunno what you've got against me, love.'

I didn't say a thing.

'Ewer angry 'bout ewer Mam and Dad. But they were over before I even . . .'

I knew he was tellin' the truth but I didn't want him tellin' me what was wrong with my Mam and Dad and me and how I was made.

'Is it? That's how I feel is it?'

He could've given up. He looked the type that would. All weak although he was well built. He didn't give up though and I had a shock.

'Look, from the minute I walk out of this lounge today, I'm 'appy to forget all the ructions tha's been between us. I can't be arsed see, with all tha'. I got a daughter, just like ew.'

Didn't expect tha' one. He's got a daughter?

'And she's givin' my ex's new man hell, too. It's really wreckin' things,' he took a big breath, 'Mine, Gemma, she's nine. She don' know no better. But you are old enough.'

Can't anyone just get on with some ironin' these days? He didn't understand after all, though he made it sound like he did at the start. The he turned to me and said,

'It's orrible, it's not nice. All this change. But I like ewer Mam enough to put up with ewer shit. So now it's up to you.' And he left the room.

From that moment on, I thought he was half decent. I never did tell him that mind. And I never did show it too much either, but I knew from that day on that he wasn't takin' the piss. He liked Mam for real and he wasn' plannin' on comin' and goin' or just goin'. And although it felt like the most cringy thing to do ever, the fact that he came in and saw me on his own showed he 'ad balls. Well, I knew he 'ad 'em anyway. Or else Mam wouldn't 'ave been after 'im.

Isn't it weird how smells bring memories back? Actually, no. That's not what I mean. Isn't it weird how smells take you back to memories? You're actually there, back there. And you can sustain it, if you keep on smellin' and smellin'. I went to the kitchen after ironin' and that-man-Terry was cookin' somethin' I hadn't smelled for years.

'What you makin'?' I asked.

76

'Corned-beef hash. Want some?' He showed the saucepan and played with the wooden spoon.

'No ta,' I said, because I didn't. But I knew that smell from somewhere else and then I remembered.

One night after school, me and Arse were walkin' back from the bus. I must 'ave been about year 8. We were supposed to go up mine, but we went up hers instead. When we walked in, we chucked our bags by the door, rippin' bits of wall paper off with the plastic catches. She made me food. Super noodles. Loved 'em then. Still love 'em actually. And then she said she wanted to show me somethin'. She took me upstairs and instead of goin' into her room, where we always went to listen to Red Dragon FM or Atlantic 252, she took me into her Mam and Dad's room. I remember askin', 'What are you doin?' and she just carried on and did big eyes to encourage me to follow.

Seein' someone else's Mam and Dad's bedroom is really weird. You feel kind of ashamed to be in there. I can't explain. The blinds were still shut and bed clothes were strewn around the place.

'Right,' she said, 'look at this.' She opened the white cupboard next to the bed and brought out a sack of things: loads of funny-sized objects – and a few toy whips and blindfolds. Were we goin' to play a game, then? Then I got real and grew up. There were at least fifteen vibrators lyin' in the bag. All colourful, like lollipops. And there were weird things there too, sharp objects and . . . I don' know. I looked at Arse all innocent and said:

'Why do they need these? What are they?' I think I knew the answer deep down only I didn't want to admit it. I'd seen things on telly, I'd read things in Just 17.

'Those things are for Mam when Dad's away,' she pointed at the vibrators matter of factly.

'And them?' I said, lookin' at all the black leather straps, all intertwined together. Like black liqorice.

'That's for when he gets back.' She smiled, closed the bag matter-of-factly, and popped it back in the cupboard. I'd never seen Arse's Dad. I knew he worked up the North of England doin' somethin', but I 'ad a horrible idea of him now. All in leather, all sweaty, all dirty. Dangerous even. I never knew why Arse showed me all these things. Maybe it was because she wanted to grow me up or somethin'. I think she wanted to show me the world. After all, we were thirteen then and she was on the pill already. And her tits were huge 'cos she took the pill. I remember bein' so jealous. I even looked at her tits when we were changin' sometimes, although I shouldn't have. Not pervin', but intrigued. Mingin' really.

Anyway, it was weird how corned-beef hash smells had brought all that back. I know why though. Because after bein' in Arse's house I came home and Dad was makin' tea, and that's what he was makin'. Corned-beef hash. He looked so clean, and normal. He was wearin' a brown woolly jumper. I gave him a hug and it felt wholesome. I had a real dad, not one that only came back in the night wearin' black leather.

Maggie texted me dinner time Saturday and asked me if I wanted to go out tha' night. Fair play, she asks me a lot. But I said no. She was on about that bloody band again. The Death of the Sales, Man! I know she's smitten with Chief but I can't think of anythin' worse that goin' to see them. Anyway, I was half expectin' Arse to phone for us to go out. She didn't, mind.

When Monday came I felt weird 'cos I knew the funeral was Tuesday. It couldn't be a normal week even if I tried. I wanted it to be a normal Monday-Tuesday-Wednesday week. Nothin' too excitin' 'appenin', and no funerals. But there was one, and it was tomorrow. I was late to the bus that mornin' and I bloody well missed it. On my way to work, I didn't listen to the walkman. I'd gone off the whole thing. I do 'ave fads sometimes and I was feelin' depressed, knowin' that it was a fad. Over in a flash. Anyway, I walked and it started to rain so I was soaked to the bone. I tried to dry off on those tiny dryers in the toilets in work but I was wet-ish all day. Damp. And my hair went all fuzzy 'cos of the rain. It's usually straight see, well, straight-ish. I've been puttin' it in a tight ponytail like that Dwynwen girl did, but there was no point after the rain. It just went all fuzzy and looked really greasy too. I wasn't 'appy. Malcometh-the-Day came over after dinner hour and asked me if I wanted to go to Union tomorrow. I said to him that I couldn't 'cos my Nanna had died and he said somethin' about Jesus and her meetin'. I thought that was quite sweet really. He also said for me to remember to come next week, 'cos I was an important member of the Union. I knew he was talkin' bollocks but it was nice of him to say somethin'.

Maggie was beamin' all day. Sayin' that Chief was out with her in Graigwen Rugby Club and she said he was all over her. I take it that's a good sign? Means love and all tha'. Or means he wants to get into 'er knickers. Where he's already been. She said the band were amazin' and that someone's thinkin' of signin' them. Maybe I was wrong about them after all. She's goin' to get t-shirts done. She's well obsessed with Chief.

I was in a really, um, what's that word, cynical, a cynical mood. I couldn't really believe tha' anyone really loved each other today. I didn't think like that everyday, but today, I did.

79

I was damp and everythin' kind of gor on my nerves. For some reason anger was bubblin' up inside me. I was glad to leave work and I thought I'd 'ave to listen to Classic FM on my walkman on the bus back 'cos I was so wound up. I got on the bus and the driver stopped me. I can't be arsed, I thought. What else is goin' to go wrong today? He said

'You, where d'you live?'

'Why?'

'I gorra know, it might not be you.'

'Be me wha'?'

'I got tonnes of people to come on, don't waste my time.'

I looked back at the queue standin' in the drizzle. Thinkin' back, he 'ad no right to force me to answer.

'Upper Porth Street,' I said, 'On the Blaena Estate.'

'It is you then. Wouldn't have thought so either,' he looked me up and down.

'What? I don't get you.'

'Someone wanted me to give you this; said give it to a girl with good skin and flat hair, but ewers is all kinky.'

''Cos of the rain,' I said and I felt really confused. I never meant to be rude to him but I snatched the piece of paper he 'ad in his hand and went to the back.

'Well, thanks a bunch,' he shouted.

I didn't think to ask who 'ad given the piece of paper. Deep down, real deep down, I knew. I just did. I opened it and I was right. It was Tellin. My heart just went, bumph. It just said: MEAT ME BY THE PARK GATES BY CUSTARDS FRIDAY 5:00. CHEERS 4 WAVIN BACK THAT DAY ;). He was so sarcastic, I could feel it in the way he'd written every word. His English was good, and if there was mistakes there, I couldn't see 'em. 'Cept he didn't spell 'meet' right. So, generally, we were on the same braininess

80

level, I reckon. I was livin' in my bubble all the way 'ome. Everythin' about tha' day had just changed in a wink. My boyfriend was about to become my real boyfriend.

I thought, God was givin' me a bit of 'ope before the funeral, 'cos God, if God is real, obviously is goin' to be around a lot for funerals, isn't He? And all the bad and irritatin' things that 'ad appened were all OK 'cos it made the little white note even more special and glittery. I thought I was in a film that night and when I got in the house, I didn't get really pissed off when I saw Terry drinkin' the orange juice straight from the carton. He pulled his mouth from it quick, in case I said somethin'. But I never. I just didn't say nothin'. Not hello, not a funny look, just a plain look and that was better than what things 'ave been like. Mam 'ad been to Lidls 'cos the floor was covered in the yellow, blue and red bags. She's started buyin' that funny German food you can buy there. I think it's 'cos she thinks Iraq is by there. Even I know that's not true. Terry said Mam was makin' frankfurter sausages and chips for tea and I never said a thing. I just went to my bedroom and lay on the bed and looked at the note.

Lyin' there, I looked at how he'd written his words. I looked at how he'd not closed his zeros for five o' clock. I felt really special and I thought how amazin' it was that he wanted to see me and how he must've liked me, even when I 'ad my Random Death with a fish finger in front of 'im. I smelled the paper and I couldn' believe that he was the one who had written it. He had held this about an hour ago. My belly flipped, and I felt things tinglin' below. My God, I couldn't believe we were goin' to go out with each other. Things were actually goin' to work out.

Excited or not, I fell asleep. I must 'ave needed it. I dreamt of funny things mind, horrible. Gareth was standin' on me and shoutin'. Nasty things like he did when he was little and wound up. When he'd get all hyper. 'Ave I got a telly on my 'ead or wha'? Stop starin!' he was shoutin'. Then he spat at me and knelt down and said. 'You've 'ad a poxy piece of paper with a note on it. Grow up. Don't look so smug, you twat. Stop lookin' like that. What d'you want? A chocolate watch?' Suddenly, I woke up shakin' my head. Spit had made a dark mark on the light blue pillow case. I felt shit. I was starvin' too. I'm always starvin' if I sleep in the day. I didn't understand why I'd dreamt of Gareth like that. Like a horrible bastard. He was wearin' his army uniform too, and the last thing I could remember, was blood pourin' from his eyes. I felt fucked up, and looked at the note again. Fuck me, I thought, I'm landed. He loves me. He fuckin' well loves me.

That night, Maggie asked if I wanted to 'ave a drink down the Legion. And I said yes. I wanted to shout Tellin's name all over the place and when we were eatin' tea, I wanted to shout the whole thing out to Mam. But I never. I just sat there, eatin' the frankfurter sausages all quiet and rosy cheeked. When Mam asked if I wanted to watch a DVD with her and Terry I said,

'No thanks, I'm gonna 'ave a drink down the Legion with Maggie.'

'Are you?'

'Aye,' I said, stuffin' a frankfurter in my mouth in case I smiled.

'Duw, what's brought all this on?'

'Nothin, thought I'd go out tonight, to get my mind off tomorrow. Nanna wouldn't 'ave wanted me mopin',' I said and smiled. I saw Terry smile at that moment too. The sod thinks I'm followin' his advice. He doesn't know about the note I've 'ad from Tellin. He was lookin' real smug and irritatin'. But I didn't say a thing. I couldn't be bothered. Let him daydream, I thought.

The drink was alright, we didn't talk much. There was a darts championship goin' on. One of the Rhondda champions was there. Daddy-o Walters. He's fat and bald and ugly too but all the girls love him, they do. 'Cos he's good at darts. Maggie and me talked for a bit and she said she had somethin' for me. She passed me a CD.

'It's the demo, the band's demo. Have a listen.'

'Thanks,' I said. Bloody marvellous. Then I drank some of my double vodka really quickly. I had to 'cos it tasted really weird. Like meat or somethin'. I prefer Smirnoff. I don' mean to be a snob, but cheap vodka's muntin'. Mulin' even. Mam has taught me that. Never buy vodka if it's not Smirnoff. But Maggie 'ad bought the drinks and so . . . Actually, I remember when we went to Majorca once, Mam bought back a case of Smirnoff from the cash and carry. Went in a flash.

I went to the toilet after downin' the vodka, and when I came out I saw in the little room by the bar, this girl kneelin' down, her face lost in Daddy-o's lap. They didn't see me, but I felt sick. Really sick. When I got back to our table, Maggie was textin' like mad. Like her fingers couldn't go fast enough. I swear they could just come loose out of her hands the speed she was goin'. I looked at her for a long time but she was takin' ages. Textin' Chief she was. Obvious wasn't it? After she finished I asked her what 'anal' was. She didn't know why I was askin' now. But Anti Peg 'ad just come to my head when I saw Daddy-o Walters bein' licked by that girl. Maggie just looked at me and her eyebrows scrunched together.

83

'You are crazy young for ewer age,' she said.

'Am I?' I said. I knew I was, but I didn't care.

'It means up the bum, mun.'

'Oh. Right,' I didn't expect that answer either. Not that it bothered me much. Anti Peg was just 'avin' a good time. Tryin' out the words she'd heard on films on bus drivers. That's wha' I reckon anyway.

'Why are you askin?' She said, lookin' back at her phone and I just said,

'It don' matter. I just thought . . . oh nothin'.'

She didn't go on, fair play to the girl. She's asked if she can come to the funeral a while back too. I don't know why she'd want to put herself through that kind of thing. She reckons it's gonna be weird for me 'cos Terry and Mum and Dad are all gonna be there. I said everythin' would be cool and she said it doesn' matter if she comes then, does it.

I went 'ome after a few. To be honest, Maggie had wound me up a bit 'cos she said that Chief and the boys (like she calls 'em – cringe) were in a practice. Suddenly, I felt like she'd used me. Wantin' to meet because Chief was busy. I hate it when girls do that.

Back home, things weren't right. Gareth was home. He was standin' by the stairs talkin' to Mam. He didn't look 'appy. He turned and looked at me and pretended everythin' was OK. His hair was different to how it used to be, all grown and more blonde. And his shoulders had gone more wide and his nose was bigger, just a touch. But I was so chuffed to see him. He looked really good lookin'.

'Well, look who it is? Little sis,' he gave me a hard kiss on my hair somewhere and then asked where I'd been. I said where and he said, 'Aye, Mam was sayin'. You got a man down there, 'ave ew? God knows, that's where everyone

84

gets their shags these days.' And he turned to look at my Mam.

I hated when things went like this. He started shoutin' again after. Like I wasn't there. It made me remember things about Mam and Dad arguin' that I never remembered before. Apparently, Dad is on anti-depressant tablets now. He shouted this, sayin' did Mam realise what she'd done to Dad. Gareth shouted and shouted. I felt a bit scared.

'Where's Terry to?' I asked Mam with spit comin' from my mouth.

'Love, go to ewer room,' she said without even lookin' at me.

'Why?' Gareth started again, 'You don't want her to hear how you've driven 'im to this? He wanted you back, after all tha' time. He wanted you back.' I knew that although Gareth was older than me, I was older in my head. He was still livin' in Nanna Land. He still thought we could all be 'appy again, together. Like the picture in the Bible. But it was never like the picture anyway. Well, not for very long periods of time anyway. There was somethin' really sad about Gareth. I could feel it. I tried not to, but I could feel it all through me. He was angry, not just angry with Mam 'cos of that-man-Terry but 'cos of more than that. He'd grown up and he didn't like it. You could tell in his eyes he'd seen things he didn't want to remember. I felt angry with him then, because I reckon he would've picked a fight about anythin' tonight. Didn't matter what, as long as he could get it out.

I was about to go to the kitchen, 'cos they were blockin' the way upstairs, when I just snapped. Gareth and Mam were screamin' and cussin' and makin' me so wound up that my head was tight. And then I exploded.

'Just shut the fuck up will you? The two of you,' They

went all quiet and I just said, 'Nanna 'aven't been put to rest yet. How do you think she'd feel seein' you two? Uh?'

I felt a bit bossy but I didn't care. I went to the kitchen to make a cup of tea and they went really quiet. Standin' there by the stairs. Next thing, I heard the front door slam shut. Gareth had gone and I had a funny feelin' he wasn't comin' back. Mam came into the kitchen. I heard her footsteps on the carpet in the corridor. I turned round expectin' her to be swearin' at me again, but she was wet with her own tears. She was cryin' really bad and it was as if she was goin' to be sick. She was retchin', like somethin' would come up, but nothin' would. I tried to give her a cwtsh, but it didn't feel right to do it for long. I tried again and then I just took her to the telly room and put some crap on. I went to fetch two cups of tea and I put about ten spoonfuls of sugar in Mam's. To calm her down, to give her energy. She was breathin' more slow when I came back with the tea and she drank it quiet.

'You've put too much fuckin' sugar in this.'

'Deliberate,' I said and she said,

'I don't like sugar in my tea, you know that.'

'I know, but you need sugar after shoutin' like that.'

'I'm sorry, love.'

'Don't worry.'

'He's angry. He wants me and ewer Dad back together.'

'I know.'

'But we're never gonna go back.'

'I know.'

'Things were shit before he got locked up, they're not gonna be better now, are they?'

'No,' I said, 'cos I knew by now she was right. No matter how long he'd been away, he'd come back the same. She'd

86

always be the same too. I could tell that just by seein' Gareth with her tonight. He's the spittin' image of Dad.

'Look Mam, don' think about this now. We need to be more chilled out tonight, tomorrow's goin' to be 'orrible.'

'I know,' she said, she turned her head and her voice went sweet, 'Did you 'ave a good time down the Legion, love?' I couldn't take her seriously because her mascara was all down her face. My Mam's face.

'Daddy-o Walters was there playin',' I said, tryin' not to say blowjob by accident.

'I heard there was somethin' goin' on down there.'

I smiled. Didn't say a thing.

'Wha's up with you, young lady? Ave you gorra boyfriend?' She was tryin' to lighten things up, through her tears, her eyes as small as beads.

Fuck, I only 'ad to 'ave a boy sayin' he wanted to meet me and I looked like I was in love.

'No,' I said, 'cos I 'aven't. Not yet. Not in real life.

Mam said then that Danny Bishop was comin' from Whitchurch tomorrow mornin' and he wanted to go in the car with us to the funeral. I was a bit confused why everyone was acceptin' this man. This stranger. Mam knew somethin' but she didn't let on. Or maybe she didn't really know anythin' at all.

'Who is this man, Mam?'

'I couldn't tell you, love. Even if I wanted to.'

I went to bed feelin' all sorts of things. Things were all tidy in my head now, with my boyfriend, even tho' I still needed to know his real name. But all the other things made me scared. Mostly, the fact that Nanna had had her secrets. You always think that ewer Nanna has been perfect or has always been old. But she's been my age. She 'ad been my age. Really, my age. Without us there. Mam was definitely hidin' somethin'. Nanna and that Danny Bishop had some history. This man I'd never met 'ad made me feel like I didn't know my Nanna. I didn't really know her more than I knew Grampa when he died. Maybe I was more grown up, and Nanna could see me big and grown, but she was old. The real Nanna or Gwen had died before then. And as I closed my eyes, I realised that I'd been sittin' with a stranger, for hours on end, every night, watchin' telly. I felt angry, I 'adn't asked her enough questions, I didn't know nothin' about her life. I'd thought that there was no more to her than Nanna, when actually, there was a lot, lot more . . .

Chapter 9

I had the guilties when I woke up. 'Cos I felt on top of the world. Or at least I did until I remembered that it was the funeral today.

I'd been dreamin' about Nanna, but that I called her Gwen, and she told me in my dream that nobody knows nobody but love can still exist. Which was quite deep for Nanna. But it wasn't her really. It was my insides tellin' me I don't ave to feel shit 'cos I found out me and Nanna didn't know each other. 'Cos we did know parts of each other, and, in the end, that's all anybody knows of anyone else.

I sat up. Confused. Then I saw the note from Tellin again. Shinin' it was. Wantin' me to read it again. Wednesday. Tomorrow, I thought. Then two days, and bang, we'll be meetin' each other. Weird isn't it? I was so excited and it sort of kept me goin' all mornin'. It was at the back of my mind, makin' me 'ang on.

Mam and Terry were in the kitchen downstairs. Terry was holdin' loads of black clothes and he was passin' them to Mam for her to iron 'em. I could see my trousers in his arms, and it felt odd. I was glad though, those trousers get hellish creased. They both smiled at me and Mam said,

'Alright love? Did ew sleep alright?'

'Yeah. Thanks.'

'Oh, well that's a relief', she said lookin' at Terry.

'Why you sayin' it like that Mam?'

'Oh, I don' know, love. Night before the funeral and all . . .' But I knew there was more to it than that.

'What Mam? Why?'

Mam wiggled in her own body, didn't want to say nothin', but she 'ad to now, didn't she.

'Well, it's nothin' really. It's just Terry popped round last night see, late. After he'd been in the Legion,' I felt scummed out. This was a mingin' situation. I didn't want to know things like that.

'And?', I said, tryin' to move on quickly.

'And, well, he heard you talkin' in ewer sleep. Said you sounded really sad, didn't you, Terr?' Terry was lookin' at the floor. Starin'.

'Everyone does talk in their sleep,' I said and looked at Terry.

'I know, love,' said Mam.

I didn't want breakfast no more. I was so pissed off. I couldn't believe Terry had heard me. I wondered then what I'd been sayin', what had I been doin'? Terry knew, and maybe Mam did too. But Terry knew. That-man-Terry who turns up and knows nothin' about me had heard me sayin' private things. Things I don't know I've said. How embarrassin? I felt really sick and I went to the shower. When I came out, I went to my room wearing my towel, and my black clothes were all hangin' up tidy on a hanger on the white cupboard. I felt really bad, guilty like. Terry and Mam had sorted everythin' out for me and I was just rude to them. I started thinkin' about me talkin' in my sleep again and I spotted the white note. Cringe, I thought. It might 'ave been about him. About Tellin. God, that would be mega cringe. I blocked it out and carried on. I needed to keep my energy today. I was sittin' by Anti Peg in the funeral supposedly, and Mam 'ad bought a bag of mint imperials for me to feed her with, to stop her from talkin' or swearin'.

Goin' in the car to the funeral was really weird. It was

like a dream. Danny Bishop was sittin' by me. First thing he'd said when he saw me was, 'Wel, Gwen fach,' which I thought was rather insultin' really. Why the fuck would I want to look like an old wrinkly woman? Anyway, he was sweet. Really crumpled up tho'. All funny dressed as well. He had like tartan trousers on and a French hat you put sideways on your head. I nearly pissed myself when I saw him first, but then his insides were so kind I couldn't help but like 'im. All the black cars followed all the black cars and then it started rainin'. Water was drippin' down the windows and it got really hot and stuffy and damp in the car. But I was glad it was rainin' to be honest. If it would've been sunny it would 'ave been well insultin' for Nanna.

The car was really quiet and I just couldn't get that joke out of my head. The one they used to ask in school. It's sick, mind. It went somethin' like this: if you found the man of ewer dreams standin' behind you in your dad's funeral and he gave you his mobile number and you lost it, what would you do? Most people said, look him up on the Internet or look in the yellow pages. But some people in school said they'd kill their mam. So that they could see 'im again, see? If you said that, you were a psychopath, supposedly. They do that test on murderers or people they think who have murdered in America. I always used to answer that I'd kill my Mam, 'cos I wanted to get the quiz right, if you get what I mean. It's a bit like those questions: two fish found dead on the floor with a patch of water and no windows – what happened? And that other one, funny one, about how you can't guess the right answer 'cos you assume that all doctors are men.

By the time I stopped thinkin' about bollocks stuff, we 'ad arrived at the chapel. There were lots of people streamin' into the place in black, and I remember thinkin' 'Who in hell's name are you?' about loads and loads of them. Mind you, they were probably thinkin' exactly the same about us. When we got out the car, we saw Gareth, Dad and Anti Peg gettin' out of theirs. They looked like the mafia and we went towards 'em. Gareth came by me and pinched my cheek. For fuck's sakes, I thought, I'm bloody eighteen, not eight. Then Mam pushed Anti Peg towards me and pushed the mint imperials into my hand. I said, 'Come on then Anti Peg,' but then I stopped. Danny Bishop was standin' by me and no one had said anythin' to him since gettin' out the car. Dad 'ad seen Anti Alison walkin' down the pavement in the rain, so I turned to Danny and said,

'You alright?'

'Right as rain,' he said lookin' up.

'Right as rain!' Gareth laughed. They both laughed. And then stopped, the same time, really quick, like as if they'd remembered they were in a funeral. I 'ad a really sore spot on my forehead, but I was glad no one was lookin' at it. It was mankin'. It was killin' me too. All red and ready to burst with white stuff in the middle. I looked at Anti Peg,

'You alright, Anti Peg. I'm gonna sit by you,' and I pointed at Danny Bishop with an open hand, 'You remember Danny don't ew? Anti Peg?'

'Sure as hell I remember that bastard', she said and he lowered his head. I didn't understand. How come she wanted him in Nanna's funeral if she hated him? Then again, come to think of it, Anti Peg was Grampa's sister so it was only normal that she wouldn't have liked 'im, if . . . If whatever. It was like tryin' to guess what was goin' on in *Neighbours* when you hadn't seen it for yonks. Gareth stood by Danny and they had a chat about the army, and I held Anti Peg's arm, stuffed a mint imperial in her gob straight away to stop her from talkin' and walked 'em into the chapel. She still managed to say somethin' tho;

'Good God on high, 'ave you seen that pimple on ewer forehead?'

The chapel smelt funny and everyone turned when we went in. It wasn't full, but it was respectable. I lost track of where Dad was, he must've been on his own. Shit, I thought. Then I thought, shit, don't swear when ewer in a chapel. Not even in your head. I looked about and saw Dad. He should have been sittin' in the pews kept for the family. Alison was lookin' for him too. I could see her. Dad's like that mind. When he should behave in a certain way, he does the opposite. It's as if he can't react in the way you're supposed to. I stared at him, tryin' to get him to notice my eyes piercin' into his face. But he didn't notice. He looked really, really bad, mind. Then again, it was his Mam's funeral. His Mam who had pushed him out from between her legs. What a weird thought. Anyway, I left Anti Peg with the mint imperials and I left Gareth with that Danny Bishop.

I went backward through the crowd and got to Dad. I grabbed him from the pew he was in and we went to sit in one of the rows in the middle that said 'Family' on big pieces of paper, and he smiled at me. Tough luck for today Dad, I thought. You're gonna just have to do as ewer told. He rested his mouth and then smiled again. A really sad, long smile. A smile so sad it could break ewer heart in two and kill you right there on the spot. I looked for Mam and Terry but I couldn't see 'em. I looked everywhere. Behind me, no one much there, 'cept I could see Maggie in the distance. She was goin' to be my friend for the funeral tea. I waved at her and smiled, and then I saw two old women twt-twtin me. I shouldn't have waved really, nor smiled, but I was really pleased to see her. Grateful. Nanna would've been happy to see me sorted. So those two old bats can go fuck themselves.

I looked for Mam and Terry again loads, until I suddenly realised where they were. They were the ones right in front of me. In front of me and Dad. Seein' the back of their heads in the row in front of me was really weird. I hadn't even recognised them. Mam had tied her hair up and I could see a mole on the back of that-man-Terry's neck. I wanted to pull it off. I don't know why, but I did. I don't like moles. Dad didn't look like he had noticed they were there so I didn't point it out. And then I thought, this row is family, it said on the paper, and that-man-Terry's not family. He shouldn't be sittin' there I thought to myself. It wasn't that I didn't like him, it just didn't seem right. Considerin' Nanna hated his guts.

The ceremony was really really borin'. Absolutely bloody awful. I didn't understand the big words the preacher used and the singin' was really crap. I don't think the preacher knew Nanna at all. He spoke with confidence although he had to look down at his notes to remember her full name. What's the point havin' a funeral, if you don't know who's gonna be sayin' all this shit about you? I must remember to sort that out before poppin' my clogs.

We sang one Welsh song. I don't remember its name but it was somethin' about livin' forever and I sang really loud on that one. Thought about how Nanna would've loved the song. Dad sang a bit but he looked like he couldn't be bothered. But he never sang the Welsh song, 'cos he couldn't speak Welsh. Weird really, that Nanna loved watchin' *Pobol y Cwm* but hadn't sent Dad nor Alison to a Welsh school. Dad didn't look bothered throughout the whole thing actually. I think he was blockin' everythin' out. In my head I was makin' up my conversation with Tellin on Friday. I'd tell him about my family, about my Nanna's funeral, about Maggie comin' over. I'd planned it all out. I knew I shouldn't say too much to him on Friday, not scare 'im away like Maggie always says she does to men. So, I thought of brainy ways of droppin' things in about myself without soundin' like I was reelin' off facts. I did that for an hour until Nanna had been carried in, carried out and cried for.

I decided in Nanna's funeral that funerals didn't mean much to me. The days before them were more important. Rememberin' the person you remembered and not sittin' with loads of damp people steamin, in a boilin' room with a man who didn't even know who had died. That was rank.

I suppose if everythin' would've come to an end after the funeral itself, it would've been an alright kind of day.

But after the funeral came the funeral tea. And that's when everythin' started goin' tits up. Nanna had always said (supposedly) that she wanted her funeral tea in the Miners' Hall. I don't know why either, 'cos Grampa hated the colliers; he worked on the trains. Anyhow, that's where we went and that's where everythin' kicked off. Dad was copin' alright for ages and he had perked up a bit too. He was jokin' to me about the fact he'd heard I had a boyfriend, which was just cringe 'cos I didn't really. Gareth and Mam came over to see him and they all had a nice chat. Mam even straightened Dad's collar which made Dad feel strange and Gareth smile. I just stood there, knowin' it didn't mean anythin'. At least, not in love terms. Terry was entertainin' Danny Bishop by the tea pots and lookin' over at the four of us, the family. Anti Peg was natterin' with a few ladies who walked away from her after about five minutes leavin' her munchin' mint imperials on her own.

When the food started comin' out, I spotted Maggie. She had been standin' in the back of the crowd textin' Chief. They were so sweet together, but they made me mad too. All lovey-dovey. Irritatin'. She came over to me and as she came over, so did Gareth. I could tell he liked her from the minute he came to talk to us. Maggie pretended she didn't notice. I'm not bein' funny, but Maggie's a funny lookin' girl. She's quite pretty and all that, but she's ugly too. I can't explain it better than that. But what always sorts everythin' out for her is her tits. They are absolutely macca and Gareth 'ad spotted 'em a while away. I left 'em talkin' 'cos I wanted to go and speak with Mam and Terry who were gettin' food. Dad and Anti Peg were standin' behind them in the queue. I pushed in front of them all and looked back at Mam and Terry.

'Alright?' I said.

'Aye,' said Mam and suddenly I realised everythin' wasn't OK.

'What's up Mam?,'

'Nothin' love. Nothin'.'

But I knew somethin' was up. That-man-Terry looked pissed off that Mam had even showed that somethin' was wrong. I went to get some volavont-thingies and some cheesy puffs. Reached too far for a tuna sandwich and then went to sit on a table on my own. I saw Mam put her plate down on the table next to me and then I saw her runnin' to the toilet. I went after her. Why was she runnin? Maybe she had the runs? When I got there, she was in a cubicle and I could hear her cryin' really quiet, and sniffin'. Hiccups and then cryin'. I couldn't stand not knowin'.

'Mam, It's me. Open the door,' and she did. Straight away, fair play to her. 'What's up?'

'Nothin' love, just, well it's been a horrible day. Nanna

gone and all.' I felt shit for doubtin' her but I knew she was lyin' through her teeth. Her mascara was all down her face and her wound-up hair was windin' down to the floor with clips everywhere.

'What's Dad said Mam? What's he said?'

'Nothin',' she sniffled.

'Yeah, he has, I can tell. Look at you.'

'Not ewer Dad, for once love. Terry.'

I didn't understand. She dribbled. I reached for some toilet roll.

'What's he said?'

'Nothin.' I passed some sheets. 'Thanks, love.'

We both left the cubicle together and stood by the sinks.

'You just said he'd said somethin'.'

'Oh fuck, look at the state of me,' she said, lookin' at her mascara-stained cheeks in the mirror.

'What did he say Mam? You got to tell me now.'

'He just thought I shouldn't 'ave played with ewer Dad's collar. I was actin' like a . . .' she stopped, 'supposedly.' God, men are so different to women.

'Dad used to be your 'usband, of course you can do that. In Nanna's funeral. He's buried his own Mam.'

'I know, love, you don't 'ave to tell me,' she said and she started cryin' again. She cries so sweet, Mam. I hate seein' her cry more than anyone. She doesn't do it a lot and she's done it twice in two days now. I tried for it not to get to me, but it did. Inevitable really.

When I got back to the room, Dad was sittin' with Anti Peg, and Terry was sittin' with Danny Bishop. They all deserved each other I thought. And Gareth and Maggie, they must've had a table somewhere else, I thought. I looked round, but I couldn't see 'em nowhere. Then I spotted

97

Maggie's bag on a chair by the tea and I went to sit by it. I couldn't see them for ages and then I started knowin', not guessin', knowin' what was goin' on. Fuck, I thought. He's spoiled everythin'. And she's a twat, I thought. I was about to get puddin', bara brith or somethin' to remember Nanna by some more, when I saw them both comin' towards me, in the light of day, from some dark corner. I just sat there on the table. I looked at them both and Gareth looked right as rain. Right as rain, I thought. Maggie looked more red-cheeked than usual and her hair was a bit more messy. She smiled a bit sheepish at me and I just thought – slag. I feel bad for sayin' it, but that's what I felt and that's what I feel now too. What a slag.

Gareth went to sit by Dad, and Maggie came back all innocent.

'Fancy some puddin'?', she asked, lookin' just shagged. 'Cos she was.

'No,' I said, although I really wanted some. I just felt really sad for Nanna, that those two 'ad been so twp and done somethin' like that, in her funeral. Then again, you couldn't blame Gareth, he hadn't seen a girl for nearly six months. But she had a choice, and she had Chief. She has Chief.

After she went up to fetch her puddin', I let her come back and sit down before I went and got mine, and I planned out to go sit by Mam and Terry. I wasn't deliberately makin' a point, I just wanted to make sure they were OK. I went and got some bara brith. A queue was startin' to come up behind me so I got some trifle too before it would be all gone. As I spooned it into my bowl, I stepped towards it to get a better grip of it. It looked lush. All squidgy and white with hundreds and thousands on the top. But I slipped, didn't I, and went head first towards the table. Shit. I dodged the glass bit of the big bowl and ended up with my head in the trifle. I tried to get up. But I kept slippin'. And I could hear some people gaspin' and others pissin' themselves. Oh, hilarious, I thought. I was strugglin' mind. I really couldn't get my head up. The bowl was stuck on me and I was slippin' all over the shop. I was drownin' in custard, and the only thing I could think was, I'll never get a chance to meet Tellin. I'll never get the chance. I tried to get a breath, but I breathed in custard and cream and I thought I was about to go and meet Nanna and Grampa, when someone grabbed the bowl and ripped it from my face. I looked up and everyone was starin'. I couldn't see them for the cream but I knew they were watchin'. Everythin' was quiet. I wiped custard and cream off one eye and the only person I could see, standin' there by me was Terry. Next thing I heard was.

'Get ewer dirty hands off my daughter. I'll handle this.'

Then while I was recoverin' from my Random Death and lickin' my lips full of custard, cream and a bit of tinned strawberry, I heard more shoutin'.

'I fuckin' saved ewer daughter's life, you cabbage.'

'Oh, so I'm a cabbage now am I?'

'No, but you *are* a mentalist.'

'Oh, is it? Is it now?'

Everyone was more quiet now.

'Well it's not me on tablets, is it, *Dad*?' Terry said and I wanted to stop them, but this was really big time serious. I knew there and then that he wasn't gettin' an answer from Dad's mouth 'cos Dad was oilin' his fist. Next thing, I heard a crisp crack on bone and I saw Terry, (or at least I think it was Terry through all the custard), fallin' to the floor and Mam runnin' over cryin'. I wanted to cry but I couldn't. I just fainted and I heard muffled voices comin' towards me. One of them was more clear that the others,

'Well Jesus, son of Mary. She's fuckin' well died on us. In her Nanna's funeral and all. And she's goin' to meet the lord with a huge fuckin' pimple on her 'ead too.'

Sharin' an ambulance with Terry wasn't nice. Mam was fussin' over us both, careful not to give one of us more attention than the other. We were like her babies. I just cried all the way there but Mam was so busy tendin' to us and askin' the ambulance driver what our pulse was supposed to be, she didn't notice. Terry noticed mind, and that made me mad. Not one of us needed that ambulance. Not one of us. And when we got there, we got sent straight from there. Well, within two hours. Terry was concussed and I was just lucky. This big, tall black man doctor just said that I was sufferin' shock and that I shouldn't go to work tomorrow. I was glad of it, and if I told the truth I acted up a bit in hospital, so that I wouldn't 'ave to go to work and so that I wouldn't 'ave to sit with Maggie after what 'ad 'appened today. One day would make the world of difference. I hoped.

And although I knew I was fine now, I couldn't help but feel that I could've died in that trifle. Mr Beynon Bioleg used to say that you could drown in a thimble full of water. And I guess the same can be said for custard.

When we got back to the house in the taxi, there was a card and flowers on the doorstep with my name on the envelope. I could tell by Terry's face, he was well jealous. And I 'ad a sneaky feelin' they would be from Tellin. I opened the envelope all quick and saw shaky old people's writin' inside. It was from Danny Bishop, the old man who knew Gwen, my Nanna. And it was in Welsh.

Chapter 10

Today I went back to work and today was Friday. Things 'aven't worked out how I planned them this week. And today was exactly the same. After Nanna's funeral, I faked a sicky so I had two days off in the end. I just couldn't face goin' back to sit by Maggie and I couldn't be bothered to face anyone after the showdown in Nanna's tea. Terry was threatenin' to press charges against Dad all day yesterday until Mam shut 'im up 'cos she realised that I thought he was serious. He was just threatenin' of course, but how would I 'ave fuckin' well known that? Dad had phoned up yesterday too, wanted to speak to Terry, said sorry, said all kinds of things. Think they sorted things out. I don't think Mam could be bothered with the whole thing. She seemed to 'ave somethin' else on her mind.

While I was off, I watched some telly and I've found a famous person who experienced a near Random Death too. That Bob Dylan bloke. There was this American documentary about him on Sky. Said he faked a near Random Death on his bike in 1966. He did it deliberate, so that he didn't have to rush around like a looney. I reckon that bloke's got his head screwed on. We should all fake a Random Death and slow the fuck down.

Anyway, apart from watchin' telly, all I'd been doin' was thinkin' about me and Tellin. Because, well, we were basically goin' out now, weren't we . . . When I went down the shop to get a Caramac for Mam, he was standin' behind me, wasn't he. He said he wanted a Yorkie, and I bought him one. As in, I actually bought it. It's in my coat pocket ready to give to him when I actually meet him later. I hope he likes it. Anyway, we walked together from the shop and he pushed me against a wall and snogged my face off. I could feel myself gettin' really turned on and then these two boys from school passed and we stopped. Now, I know this all happened in my head, but it all felt really real. I even pushed myself against the brick wall to imagine how it would feel. He is an amazin' lover, I knew he was goin' to be. Mind you, I'd decided the minute I saw Maggie comin' back from bein' with Gareth that I wasn't gonna sleep with Tellin straight off. That would be bad, although I wanted to. I knew I wanted to, and I knew I'd love it. 'Cos, well, in a way we'd already done it. In my head.

Anyway, all the time I was off work, although I watched some telly, I 'adn't been on the sofa all the time like I was used to. I hadn't been lyin' there, feelin' sorry for myself. Watchin' *This Morning* after Jeremy Kyle. Sometimes I went to my bedroom and lay on the bed listenin' to Welsh radio. I'd had a funny turn after that man Danny Bishop sent me those flowers. Mam had put the flowers out all nice in a vase on my bedside table. The little card I had with a tulip on the front was lyin' right next to the note from Tellin. I felt weird listenin' to Welsh radio, because no one else in the house understood it. I felt brainy. But the daytime stuff is borin', it's for old people, so I turned it off after a while.

I reached for the card from that Danny Bishop. I read it again. It was so sweet of 'im, to write anythin'. He didn't need to send me flowers. But he did. His note said, 'Roedd dy Fam-gu mor falch dy fod ti'n gallu siarad Cymraeg. Brysia wella'n fuan, Danny.'

It said that Nanna was 'appy I went to a Welsh school. Gareth went to a Welsh school too, I thought. Weird that he pinpointed me out. It was funny tho', 'cos Nanna never said much to me in Welsh. Always watched Welshy stuff, but never really spoke it to me. Until I had tha' 'lectric shock. But then I started thinkin', fuck me, they obviously knew each other quite well, Danny Bishop and Nanna, 'cos she'd told him that she was chuffed I was in a Welsh school. That's quite a big deal. So, they must've been in contact over the years. And, I suppose they spoke Welsh together. I couldn't even imagine how they would have met. Nanna came from up here and he lived in Witchurch down Cardiff way. I racked my brain that day, what did Nanna used to do? I didn't really know if she ever had a job. I asked Mam after, but she shrugged her shoulders and said somethin' about bein' a cleaner. A cleaner, I thought. Well, that didn't explain it. And then Mam said, 'Down Cardiff, a cleaner down Cardiff way.' And I remember her lookin' at me then, as if she could read my mind. Mams are weird like that. She could tell that I was tryin' to figure things out. But she didn't say anythin' else.

Anyway, it was 'cos of that card that I decided to listen to the Welsh radio. What's more, I decided to write Danny a letter in Welsh too. It took me ages, and I was strugglin'. And you know what's shit? I never finished it either. I felt like a right twat for tryin' to write in Welsh so I scrumpled it up and threw it in the bin. To be honest, I can be like that. Really obsessed with somethin' one minute and then give up the next. I was like that with the saxaphone in Blwyddyn 8. I took it up 'cos it was free and I wanted to play the Pink Panther theme tune. But by the third lesson, I felt all out of enthusiasm because I'd understood you had to practise.

So Thursday was a dull and borin' day. A day of lyin' about, a day of givin' up on a few things. A day of realisin' that I wouldn't be able to do anythin' I wanted in life because I was me. And bein' eighteen means I've got some hang-ups already. So, yeah, yesterday was a well depressin' day. But in a way I knew that God was preparin' me for an excitin' Friday. He was givin' me the calm before the storm. I know that He does that. If He exists, and if He's a He.

When I got up today, I 'ad all butterflies in my stomach. I also 'ad the shits for about half an hour before leavin' for the bus. I looked at Tellin's note again to make sure I met 'im in the right place. Weirdly, I started to have those jitters. You know when you're convinced that someone's bullin', havin' a laugh. I nearly started doubtin' the whole thing. And then I remembered the way I felt when I'd played with myself yesterday in bed. I hadn't done that much before, but I'd seen it in a film. And it felt good, and it felt right with him doin' it. In my head. So that's what did it for me, I knew we were meant to be and that he wanted to meet me. Fuck knows how I was so confident about it, but once I'd psyched myself up, there was no turnin' back.

I straightened my hair, and put a top on that showed my boobs, but only a bit. I looked in the mirror and pulled my straightened hair back tight in a ponytail. Like that smart bird had done. That smart bird who came from the Welsh Language Commission. Shit, I don't remember her name now. What was it? Heulwen? No, shit, I couldn't remember.

Anyway, this mornin' when I got on the bus, the driver looked at me funny.

'Good God, I nearly didn't know you. You've got slap on . . .'

'Aye,' I said, paid and ran up the back of the bus. I was a bit pissed off with what he'd said actually. I mean, I hadn't made that much of an effort today. It just made me realise how much of a minger I must usually look on my way to work. I decided there and then I would make a bigger effort

104

from now on, every day. A bit of make-up, straighten my hair. That type of thing.

Seein' Custards from a distance made me nervous. I hadn't been in work for a while and I felt like I hadn't been there at all the last few weeks. My life 'ad just taken over. Anyway, when I got in to the yard where people park their cars for Custards I saw Chief comin' out of his car. I felt awful guilty 'cos of what 'ad appened between Maggie and Gareth. He didn't look 'appy mind and I could tell he knew.

'Alright Chief?'

'Not bad', he said, walkin' towards me and brushin' his hair out of his eyes.

'What's wrong?'

'Oh, I think you know love.'

'Do I?' I asked, tryin' not to look him in the eyes. He's the one usually like that.

'Yes, I think you do.'

'I'm sorry. It's nothin' to do with me.'

'Isn't it? I heard it was a lot to do with you.'

'How come? I'm so sorry.' I was gettin' major confused. I didn't get what he was telling me at all.

'We've had loads of complaints, well three.'

''Ave you?' I asked. He wasn't on the same wavelength as me.

'Yes we have. People in Cardiff, they've been phonin' up sayin' the message on our lorries is wrong in Welsh. It's written bad.'

I just stood there. I wanted to cry. I was blushin'. I knew I was blushin'. I could feel my cheeks burnin' up. Red and hot.

'Is it?' I asked with a squeaky voice, tryin' not to let my lips shake. Once my bottom lip went, I knew I'd start cryin'.

105

'That Doonwhen girl is comin' in again this afternoon. She'll 'ave a word with ew. Alright?'

Dwynwen, I thought, that's her bloody name. And then I thought, oh fuck. Dwynwen's comin' in and she's gonna give me a bollockin'. She's goin' to be so disappointed. I just walked past Chief then and went straight to the toilet. I went into a cubicle and rolled myself up in a little ball in the corner. I was so embarrassed that I just bawled my eyes out. Maybe I wasn't perfect, but I didn't say I was. And I hadn't tried for a job as a translator. It had just, well, sort of happened. I was angry and upset that this week was just like hell to me. The only thing that kept me goin' was thinkin' about meetin' Tellin tonight. God was givin' me shit so that I would appreciate when somethin' good 'appened to me. I knew that that's what it was.

When I got to my desk Maggie was there. I'd hoped she'd be off work ill or somethin'. I'd 'oped I would be able to get away with another day of not rememberin' how disappointed I was with her. When I saw her the first time, the only thing I could see was her and Gareth shaggin', like dogs. I could see it in front of my eyes. It was mulin'.

'Mornin',' she said, all awkward.

'Aye, mornin',' I said.

'You been cryin?' she asked all interested.

'No,' I said. I wasn't gonna tell her. I wasn't. I kept goin' until dinner and then when I got back to my desk she was there again, only this time she gave me a post-it note.

'Chief wanted me to give you this.' She looked at me hard, when she said Chief. It was really awkward. I hated it. The note said 'Doonwen comin' 2 o' clock'. I looked at my watch. It was 1.50 so I just upped and left.

I went to the toilet on my way to see her. To sort my head

106

out, and my hair. I dabbed a tissue on my eyes to get rid of the mascara shadows. I messed with my hair. And I heard my phone bleep. I checked it: it was Arse.

'Alex n me fnshd. Wntd me 2 tk it up the arse all the tm. Out soon?x'

I couldn't help but laugh. With her name bein' Arse and all. I remembered how we used to share a fag butt in Nisien (that was like a block of classrooms in school). Mr Williams found us once, and we ran like banshees to the school garden. Behind a bush there, where we found a used condom, we swapped friendship bracelets. I remember that like yesterday. I didn't know where the fuck those bracelets had gone, but they were still on our wrists, really. I got sent out of Coginio that afternoon too, because I'd been speakin' English with Ed Bourne. That was a bad patch lookin' back, just when Dad got into trouble the first time.

Suddenly, I found myself back in the toilets in Custards. Amanda from accounts came in and said hello. She's lovely she is. Just had her fortieth. Smart for her age. Hope I'll be like that. Right, I thought, Dwynwen, and I walked out taller than I went in. Even if I did feel like shit 'cos I knew she was goin' to give me a bollockin'. I knew too that the company 'ad spent thousands on the new bloody signs. Once again, I smelled her before seein' her. The same, lovely smell. All perfect like before.

I went into the room and she was there. She had all brown clothes on but, instead of lookin' mankin' as anyone else would in a brown suit, she looked amazin'. My hair was tied back like the ponytail she had before and she had wavy hair now, down to her shoulders. I felt like a prick. But her smell made me feel better. All expensive and all womanly.

'Ishte,' she said, 'sdim angen i ti fecso. Ma' fc'n olreit.'

Fair play to her, she didn't need to say that. She wasn't goin' to be mad at me. She explained after a while that she was mad with Custards. She said they shouldn't ever 'ave given me so much translatin' work. She told me I could be a translator, if I did courses and an A-level in Welsh. I started sweatin': I didn't want to fuckin' do that. I said I was sorry to her, I said I never chose to be a translator and I said that I never wanted to be one again. She said that she'd found out because a letter had been sent to the Commission by some twat in Cardiff. Except, she didn't say he was a twat. She said she didn't usually do visits about things like this, but she said she liked me and she wanted to explain things and try and help. I felt mega chuffed in a way. As if I'd done all this deliberately for her to say she liked me.

I told her I wanted to speak Welsh, and that I'd tried with people on my street but it didn't work. I said it didn't work like that up here. I got a bit angry I think and she just said,

'Wy'n gwbod. Wy'n gwbod.' She knew damn well there was no way I could practise speakin' Welsh with anyone I knew. For a minute, I thought she was gonna do an 'Annie' on me. Offer to adopt me and speak Welsh to me for ever, or meet up with me to practise my Welsh or do somethin'. But she didn't. She couldn't. She couldn't do anythin'. She just kept sayin', 'I know, I know' all the time. Once she'd made sure I didn't ever want to be a teacher, which I fuckin' well don't, she stood up, laughed and said, 'Diolch, Sam'. I said, thanks for what, and she said, 'Diolch am fod mor onest.' She had a really funny, sad look in 'er eyes. I reckon she thinks I'm on drugs.

I felt like shit after leavin' the meetin' with Dwynwen because I knew that would be the last time we'd meet. I knew I'd let her down too and that made me feel even worse.

But, when I went back to sit by my desk, Maggie was there and all the memories of her shaggin' Gareth came rushin' back. Dwynwen had gone, and things were back as they were.

I sat lookin' at my computer for the rest of the day. I should have been doin' spot checks on the powdered custard but I felt as if the world was against me. I felt as if Chief had betrayed me, although I knew it was my own fault that the Welsh was wrong on the lorry signs. I just sat there wonderin' whether I had anyone left to go to my funeral, if I ever had one. I was so pissed off with the world that afternoon I just wanted to escape to another country. Except somethin' was keepin' me goin'. Like a little treat in the back of my head. Keepin' me from fuckin' killin' someone. I had a date to go on.

It was four o' clock by the time I looked at the clock and I felt my heart go. My God, I thought. One hour. I ran to the bathroom to try and doll myself up. I'd nicked Mam's mascara to put on and I tied my hair up really tight again 'cos it had gone more loose. As I was doin' all this, Maggie came in. Shit, I thought. I didn't want to be sharin' the same space as her. It made me cringe out.

'Ooh, look at you. Where you goin' after work then?'

'Nowhere,' I said. I couldn't bare it anymore. Maybe she was a slut, but I had no one to talk to in this place.

'Shurrup you knob! It's obvious you're meetin' some boy,' she shouted at me.

And I told her about Tellin. Really quick, with no fuss.

'Oh, that's dead romantic.'

I always thought that was a funny one too. Dead romantic. I looked at her and smiled. Yes, I s'pose it was quite romantic. I didn't really want to be best friends or

109

anythin' but I didn't see no harm in tellin' her. She disappeared into one of the cubicles and I stared at myself in the mirror. My eyes looked weird, my ears looked lopsided. But I smiled again, with only me there. Dead romantic.

By the time I was at my desk again, it was half four. I had shit loads of things to do but I couldn't be bothered. I just sat there thinkin' about Tellin's lips, his cheeks and the way we'd kiss for the first time. Although, it obviously wasn't the first time in my head. The translatin' folder on the desktop just seemed to stand out like a sore thumb, throbbin'. Remindin' me I was shit. Five o' clock. Bloody hell. It was five. I stood up and went. Maggie said good luck and I said thanks, I needed it. She was all smiley. Happy that I was happy I think. I said 'Bye' and off I went. I didn't feel guilty for speakin' to her again. I didn't feel as if I was usin' her either. She owed me one after the mess in Nanna's funeral. So, it was OK for me to have the upper hand for a while.

Now, the park gates are about two minutes from work so I walked slowly. I didn't want to be the first one there, did I? I couldn't do that. I wanted to be fashionably late. Cool like. I got there, five past, and he wasn't there. Bugger, I thought, I'm gonna look sad now. Like a loner. I stood there for another ten minutes, but he still hadn't arrived. I looked at my watch. I was still excited. Couldn't breathe nearly. All nervous. Quarter past. I started to get a bit cold and some people passed me, lookin' funny at me. I couldn't wait to turn round and see his green eyes sayin' hello. I waited, and then suddenly, I saw the back of his head on the other side of the street. I wanted to wave my hand but I couldn't. And good job I didn't in the end, because it wasn't him.

When it got to half five I started thinkin' awful things. He was playin' a joke on me? It wasn't him who wrote the note?

110

Maybe he'd said to meet some place else? I was really confused and it was startin' to get darker. I stood there wishin' the note had said 5:30. But it didn't. I knew it said 5. I felt so ill. So sad. When it came to quarter to, I knew I would 'ave to go. I felt betrayed and I felt like a mug. What type of girl would just see someone once and then fall in love? What type of girl would fall for such a shit joke? Nasty I thought, with tears wellin' up in my eyes. Fuckin' well nasty. That's a foust of a thing to do. But this couldn't be, I thought, because we've already kissed, in my head. And I've heard him breathe. I've tasted him. I started breathin' in a panic and I felt sick too.

I ran from the gates to the bus stop. It started pickin' rain and I could see the gates from there. I knew he hadn't been over there since I'd gone, and I knew deep down, by now, that he wasn't goin' to be there either. Finally, I saw the bus come down the hill. It was shinin'. It was like a carriage in a fairytale, or a film. My carriage to take me home, I thought. Back to safety, and away from all this. When I got on the bus, the same driver I had this mornin' was still drivin'. Christ. And when I sat on the big white bus, I felt more awful than I'd felt all day. I'd wanted the bus to make me feel normal again. Make me forget what I was doin' here in the first place. But it didn't. It hit me harder than ever before. He hadn't turned up. Tellin. Tellin. He hadn't come. I hadn't tasted him. I had been dreamin' this in my head. I'd been wishin' it, not livin' it. All awful feelins of missin' someone turned my stomach and drained me of everythin'. All horrible feelins of knowin' that none of what had happened so far was real. Not really real. I felt mental, but I also felt like I missed him.

And for one minute, on that bus back home, I nearly didn't want to live anymore. And I never feel like that. Never will again maybe. But for that one moment, on the bus, I nearly couldn't be bothered to carry on. And people would have thought I was petty. Wantin' to quit life because of one stupid crush gone wrong. But that's honestly how I felt. As low as you can go.

When I got off the bus, the driver looked me up and down and smiled sweetly.

'Yes, and here you are. 'Ad a good time did you? Met your special man?' and he winked.

'Hm', I said, tryin' my hardest to smile.

'Young love innit, bach,' he said lookin' at all the old women standin' behind me and they all did that 'Oh' sound and then looked at me all gooey. They all had Nanna's face tonight. Every damn one. I was freaked out. I wanted to bang their heads together. I stepped off the bus and kept my head down. I wanted to cry my guts out, but I didn't have the energy. I felt so ashamed of myself. I'd let myself down. I'd been too keen, I'd let myself believe somethin' that wasn't true. Like when I used to dream how Mam and Dad would get back together.

When I got in the house, Terry and Mam came from the television room.

'Oh love, you're home. Where've you been?' She looked at me and saw bits of mascara all over the shop. 'Where've you been love?,' she asked, a bit concerned this time.

'Nowhere,' I said.

'Well,' said Terry, 'we've got some good news after the week we've all had.'

We've all had, I thought. Wharerver. He didn't even know Nanna.

'What's that then?'

Mam looked at me with big, big eyes. Her cheeks were

really really rosy, they reminded me of Tellin's and they made me realise what was goin' on. She was bloody well pregnant. I could tell. You can tell in some womens' faces. 'Specially ewer Mam's.

'I'm pregnant,' she said and it wasn't such a shock bein' as I'd guessed it. I wanted to be 'appy. I wanted to say how good I felt about it all, but I didn't 'ave no energy and I was the saddest person who'd ever walked the planet. I wanted to smile, I really tried. And I did smile, but it turned into cryin'. I hated cryin' in front of people. But I also felt angry. My Mam, fuckin' well pregnant, what the fuck?

'I'm sorry. I'm glad. I am. It's just, I've had a shit day. I'm really happy. How long 'ave ew known?'

'Three months gone love.'

'Oh right,' I said, then I realised, 'Three months?'

They must've been seein' each other ages before Mam said anythin' to me. Christ. As I walked away, my mobile bleeped twice. Normally, I feel excited when that happens. Who could it be, and so on. But today, I couldn't give a shit. I went upstairs and Mam tried to come after me. I turned to look at her, with mascara drippin' everywhere, and my nose runnin'. I knew it was runnin'. I could feel it.

'I'm arlight, I just wanna sleep.'

She listened and turned back. I was so cold inside after standin' about for such a long while outside. I was shiverin'. As I walked up the rest of the stairs I remembered I should say one thing to Mam and Terry, so I did.

'By the way, I still think ewer too fuckin' old to 'ave a baby.'

And before either of 'em 'ad a chance to say somethin' back, I was gone. Round the corner and into my bedroom.

Past Nanna's bedroom, her door wide open and her bed made all tidy.

For a bit, I sat on the bed starin' at nothin'. I looked at my phone and I saw two messages flashin'. Maggie and Arse. They always text me the same time these days. Somethin' must remind them of me. Weird. Anyway, the first message was from Arse, sayin' she was still up for goin' out, and askin' how my 'man' was. I wanted to text her back, 'He doesn't exist', but I never. I just deleted the message. I didn't have the energy. My second text was from Maggie. She was obviously tryin' to make an effort now. 'Hope things are goin' good wiv u and the boy. Wanna go see 'D.O.T.S.M' weekend? Mx'. How many times did I have to text her back with excuses? I didn't want to see that bloody band, and I knew that I couldn't look Chief in the eyes from now on either. How the fuck she could is another thing.

I decided I'd get into bed and just close my eyes tight. Maybe I could close them so tight that I wouldn't have to think about any of this shit. So tight, that all the world couldn't seap in between the gaps. So tight that I could switch it all off. So tight, that I didn't even know if the curtains 'ad been drawn or not.

I opened them again because the only thing I could see when I closed my eyes was Tellin's face. His green eyes starin' back at me. The hurt was thumpin' my head. I loved him. I love him. I'm sure I do. I reached for Tellin's note and read it again. I think my twisted head had hoped that I hadn't understood the note properly. The one final hope I had left. I ripped it to shreds and threw all the little bits of white paper on the floor. Some stuck to my finger but I brushed them off. I ripped it 'cos I was so angry that I'd trusted such a tosser. I was angry 'cos I knew now that nothin' of it was real. I cried then, for a bit. I didn't change into my pyjamas. I just lay in my clothes. What was the fuckin' difference between pyjamas and clothes anyway? Fuck all, when you're feelin' like this.

I closed my eyes and wished sleep so hard that it came. And when it did come, like a big wave draggin' me out to sea, I didn't 'ave to think about a thing.

In the middle of the night, I woke because someone was pullin' my bed clothes. It was Tomtom. Usually, I kicked him off or shouted. But I just left him this time. Somehow, I was glad of the company. And I had this really weird feelin' that Tomtom knew what I was goin' through. Maybe Nanna had sent him here to look after me tonight. Or maybe he was a cat just lookin' for a mat. Either way, I didn't care.

Chapter 11

When I woke up this mornin' I 'ad a head ache like I don't know what. I got up and I looked through the window. That's all I saw was mist and rain and a magpie. One for sorrow I thought, and then I thought to myself, 'Well ewer too fuckin' late, my love. I've felt it all, and you comin' is never gonna make things worse. Because things couldn't get any worse.'

They are pretty mind. Magpies. All black and white and always clean lookin'. And weirdly, although I felt shit today, I also 'ad some humour in me. Somethin' dark, somethin' that just got me to wake up and get on with things. I dunno if this is true, but sometimes I think ewer body knows when you're gonna experience bad things. What I'd been thinkin' about when I woke was, how I couldn't believe I'd been led to think that Tellin was for real. I don't know how, I'm not usually fooled like that. It came real slow over me that I'd tricked myself, that I'd willed it to happen so much that I just ended up lovin' someone. Makin' them up even. Actually makin' someone up. Although, if I'm honest, I'm still convinced that he did love me. Or maybe I'm still just fucked up. If I told a psychiatrist or a doctor all this, they'd lock me up, cert.

I knew that if I'd 'ave to see 'im, I'd fuckin' well murder him. I was sometimes scared of the fact that I felt I could kill someone, with my bare fuckin' hands. Once, when Gareth bit Nanna until blood came from her hand when he was refusin' to come in from playin' football, I remember thinkin' I could kill him. I remember imaginin' me pushin' him up against the cupboard and fetchin' a knife. The only thing that stopped me was that I knew I'd feel shit after. I pretty much knew I would feel good and excited while doin' it. Acutally teachin' him a lesson. I tried to think about somethin' else, I hated thinkin' of things like this.

Suddenly, I'd made myself feel worse than ever. Not only had I imagined my boyfriend and our break-up but I was also thinkin' about killin' people. I was a murderer in the makin'. Or maybe everyone is . . .

Maggie had texted me in the night when I was sleepin', 'well?x'. I knew it: she thought I'd had the best shag of my life last night. I didn't answer. I just turned the phone off. It was Saturday, I could do as I fuckin' well pleased. A Saturday and feelin' shit. But it didn't matter which day it was. It was a crap day. I went downstairs in my pyjamas and went straight to the kitchen. Over the past few weeks I've been changin' before goin' to fetch breakfast because of that-man-Terry. But today, I couldn't give a toss what he thought or saw.

When my cuppa was ready, I turned around and Mam was standin' there in the kitchen. She looked at me. I turned around and threw my teabag into the sink.

'Not in the sink love, you know how much I hate that.'

I didn't move it, I just turned around. I thought – she knows somethin's wrong, 'cos Mams always do. But you know what, she didn't see it this time. Either she was too wrapped up about the baby or I was a really good actress. The baby, I thought. Bloody hell, I hadn't had time to think about that one. Of course, I thought, she was too wrapped up in herself. And that's fine, that's fair enough. Mam started talkin'. I felt so tired; I didn't even catch what she said to start.

'. . . so what I was thinkin' love was. Are you listenin' to me?'

'Aye,' I said.

117

'Good. Well, basically, don't tell Gareth about the baby, right, love?'

'Alright,' I said, hardly listenin'.

'He's goin' back tonight and he's got enough on his plate. Ewer Dad doesn't know either. He'll blow his top. So . . .'

'I know, I won't say a word. D'you think I'm tha' thick?'

'Gareth's goin' back so we're 'avin' dinner here at one, alright? He's comin' over. You better be 'ere, not out gallivantin'.'

I gave her a weird look. When was I ever out galli-fuckin-vantin'? I went to fetch some orange juice. I'd had a real cravin' all of a sudden. Just for a drink. Cold. I opened the fridge and got the carton.

'There's nothin' in it,' I said.

'Isn't there?'

'Where's it all gone then?'

'I don't bloody well know, do I!' she said, but I knew it was that-man-Terry who'd drunk it. And that was the final straw. That-man-Terry, paradin' about, thinkin' he owns the place, drinkin' the orange juice. The worse thing was the fact that he'd left an empty carton in the fridge. Mam saw the look on my face.

'O, grow up, mun. You've got a face like a munter on ew.'

'Mam, it's the golden rule. You never fuckin' leave an empty carton in the fridge. That's like not puttin' a new toilet roll out when you finished the last one.'

She could tell I was just gettin' all my anger out on Terry. What made me really mad was the fact that she just laughed and walked out. A big hearty, irritatin' laugh. My blood boiled up.

'What's so fuckin' well, fuckin' funny?!' I shouted really,

really loud. And she didn't even answer back. She never even said, 'mind ewer language, young lady'. She just left me in the kitchen with an empty orange juice carton in my hand. Lookin' pathetic. Mam was goin' down Lidl's to get more random food for Gareth's dinner and she wasn't goin' to let me spoil her life. In a way I felt – good for you. In another way I felt – piss off then. Go an' 'ave ewer new baby and ignore me then, you slag. I felt both those things at exactly the same time. I felt confused and so angry. Standin' there in my pyjamas with a cup of tea and an empty orange juice carton.

Before Gareth came for his dinner and went back to Iraq, I went down the shops. I don't know why I did it really. I never do that but I thought I might see Tellin. I knew that if I saw him, I could ask him why he did what he did. Secretly, I just wanted to see him though. I wanted him to explain to me why he'd had this last-minute thing creep up. I wanted him to say sorry. I wanted him to hold my hand. That's all. I just wanted to see him. I'd be 'appy if that's all that would 'appen even. Just seein' him. I got changed first, though. And in my bedroom, that mornin' I did somethin' cringe. I know that boys do this thing called blind man's wank. They sit on their arm until they have a dead hand and then they wank, and imagine it's someone else. Well I did that, only a bit different. I sat on my hand while I was listenin' to Vernon Kay. Then, when it went numb, I held it in my other hand. For a moment, with my eyes closed, I imagined it was Tellin's hand, holdin' mine.

I soon came to my senses once I went down the shops, where I didn't see no one I knew. 'Cept Malcometh-the-Day with a big sandwich board sayin', 'God is this way'. Weirdly, he was sittin' right in front of the bettin' shop. I thought I better point this out to him. But I couldn't be bothered. He'd only 'ave said somethin' like 'It's where He's needed the most.' I love it when crazy religious people say things like that. They've got an answer for everythin'.

When I got back from town I was a real mixed bag of feelins. Feelin' really depressed and really happy, feelin' safe and mixed up at the same time. Dad opened the door to me, which was well weird. It was like old times 'cept he had less hair and I never went out anywhere for him to open the door for me when he lived with us. So I s'pose it wasn't like the old times at all really.

Dad, Mam, me, Anti Peg and Gareth sat there eatin' all weird German stuff from jars and Gareth struggled to get anythin' down. Excited about going back to Iraq, I suppose. Or dreadin' it. Why had Mam made all this random, foreign food when all Gareth really wanted was sausage with mash and jam rolly-polly with custard? Terry was standin', servin' up all the potatoes from the saucepan. Dad was lookin' up at 'im. Dad behaved himself, fair play. He wanted to fuckin' lamp Terry, mind, I could tell.

Tomtom was lookin' up at the table, sniffin'. Peg had Flo on a lead in the telly room, because Tomtom and her didn't get along at all. But she'd insisted on bringin' her and that was fair enough. She loves that dog.

I felt weird knowin' there was a baby in my Mam's belly and that half the people on the table didn't know. Until I noticed suddenly, that Anti Peg had clocked. She was as subtle as a brick, but still no one twigged, 'cept me and Mam.

'Well, fuck me. Ewer lookin' healthy, Janet.'

'Aye,' Mam said and pointed at the German food with 'er fork, 'er mouth full of food. She spat some words out then,

120

'All this foreign food from Lidls see Peg. It's bloody good for you. Good for ewer bowels.'

Peg just looked at Mam.

'And two rosy cheeks you've got too. Anyone more twp than me would think you were pregnant.'

Mam laughed and no one said nothin'. It was too stupid to be true. Dad didn't look up and that-man-Terry didn't even flinch, which made me think he was a dab-hand at lyin'. Peg looked at Mam and Mam swore at her with her eyes.

After that there was this weird, foreign pastry puddin' and custard from Custards. Dad was awful quiet and Gareth was major quiet. All the women were laughin' and talkin'. That was pretty normal in our house. The men eatin' and the girls 'avin' a chat. Mam asked if anyone wanted more of the pastry. No one did 'cos the stuff was mingin'. Mulin' in fact. She pushed it on Gareth then, who said 'No thanks'. She pushed it on 'im again sayin',

'You need ewer energy now love. Come on, tuck in, for Mam.' Then it happened. Gareth just threw his bowl of puddin' against the wall and it smashed all over the place. He started shakin', spit comin' from his mouth and snot from his nose. Custard dribbled down the wall. Yellow, yellow custard on the brown wall. He put his hands on his head and started cryin'. Leanin' on the table. He cried, and then he shouted and said,

'I heard it again. I don't want to fuckin' go back. Please don't send me back. I don't want . . .' He cried all childish and screamed. I was scared. Really bad. Terry took Anti Peg to the telly room and they just let me sit there.

Gareth stood up then and started smashin' the place up. He threw the picture of Nanna off the cupboard and Mam screamed. Then he picked a jug up, a see-through glass jug.

Mam went towards him, but Dad stopped her. He didn't want her to get hurt. I don't know what came over Gareth but he just threw the jug straight at Tomtom who was sleepin' in the corner of the room by then, after he'd 'ad his fill of weird German meat. The glass smashed on his belly, he woke up and then just made a cat screamin' noise. His belly was ripped and I could see the glass had broken in deep. His guts were 'angin' out. I wanted to cry now. I felt so sad. I knew he was goin' to die and I knew that Nanna would be cryin' now, lookin' down. Mam just screamed again and put her hands on her eyes. She didn't want to even see it. It looked mingin'. There was no point me pickin' him up, he was dyin'. Dad just sat there and folded his arms over his head, like a scared teddy bear. I just sat there, nearly as if I wasn't in the room. Everythin' was movin' in slow motion. I couldn't cope.

'I can't fuckin' see them again. Their fuckin' faces and their fuckin' blood. Everywhere. And I can't, I can't go. No one can force me. I , I , I don' know . . .'

He kept repeatin' himself and he smashed the window in the cabinet. Blood went down his knuckles and Mam was screamin', out of voice nearly. Don't Mam, I thought, 'cos of the baby. But she screamed, really high pitched. Gareth's ill, I thought. I could see when I looked in his face that he was seein' other things in that room. He was seein' other rooms. He wasn't even in a room. Mam tried to calm 'im down but in the end he only stopped 'cos he was so tired he couldn't do no more damage. Dad was quiet for ages and then he raised his head and said to Mam,

'He's been 'avin' nightmares.'

Mam looked at Dad and I could see they wanted to cry their bellies up their throats. Their hearts were swelled big and they wanted to cry like babies. But they couldn't.

Mam spluttered spit and tears,

'Well, why the fuck 'aven't you told me all this before?'
She looked at Dad all angry, spittin' the word 'fuck' out of
her mouth as if it were a bullet.

I went to make tea and I put ten sugars in Gareth's. By
the time I came back, he was just bleedin' on the little chair
by the cupboard with his head in his lap. He was still cryin'
mind. But he was like a little boy now. I tried not to look
down at Tomtom. He was lyin' there with his mouth open
and his eyes frozen. Fixed in one place. Blood and guts and
dirty stuff were oozin' out of his belly and I felt sick. I
couldn't cry or do anythin'. Somethin' or someone just gave
me this weird energy to turn into a robot and just do things. I
wasn't feelin' nothin', I was just numb.

Gareth didn't go back to Iraq after that. A man came at 3
o' clock, from Cardiff. He runs the place for ill soldiers in
Wales. He said Gareth would be right as rain soon. Right as
rain, I thought.

I was with Mam all night after that, but she just stared
at the wall. She wasn't goin' mental or anythin' but she
didn't 'ave any energy to do anythin' else, that's all. I just
sat there thinkin' about eraser pens. Those pens we 'ad
in school. Everyone thought they were well cool. The white
tip got rid of the fountain pen mistakes and the other side
of the pen was blue, and with that bit you could write a
new story. I wanted to use a big fat eraser pen over last week,
and just write in – normal week, nothin' 'appened. But
I couldn't. And anyway, Mrs Cadwaladr always used to
nick those off us because she thought we were wastin' time.
Cow.

When I went to bed that night, weirdly, I didn't feel too
gloomy. I think it's 'cos when the shit hits the fan, you've got

to get off your arse and sort things out. You just 'ave to. And when someone's worse off than you, you just cope. Maybe it was me and the strength I had without knowin' but maybe it was strength I'd been given by God, or by Nanna, or from the weird German food. I felt determined goin' to bed, I was gonna do somethin' with my life. I had nothin' to lose, 'cept a few pounds. I could do anythin'. Weird thing was I felt really dark thoughts at exactly the same moment as when I felt like I had hope. I kept tryin' to block out thoughts of Gareth in a straight jacket in that soldier place. I kept havin' to block out pictures of Tomtom squashed tight in an old Clarks shoebox in the pantry. I just had to block them all out and think normal stuff.

Mr Vaughan in school always said there was no word in English for *hiraeth*. I remember that because I had hiraeth for Neil Griffiths in school at the time. I fancied the pants off of him. The closest word in English is 'yearning', I think. I don' quite remember either. But anyway, in bed that night, I had hiraeth, real big *hiraeth*. I wanted to see somethin' nice happenin'. I had *hiraeth* for things to turn out OK again. Deep down in my belly, so deep I couldn't tell anyone where it was exactly. I wanted to hear someone say a happy story and, after the happy story, I wanted to here someone say 'The End.' Like when Mrs James used to say 'Y Diwedd' at the end of *amser stori* on the carpet in primary school.

I looked at the roof of my bedroom and at the little glow-in-the-dark stars on the roof. I'd put them up years ago. They were well cool them. They were shinin' in the dark and they were sayin, 'Fuck it Sam, you'll be alright, and so will Gareth, in the end.' I just put my head down. I hadn't thought about Tellin at all since Gareth had 'ad his turn. And then I thought, really selfishly too, that God 'ad given me

124

somethin' worse to worry about so I wouldn't have to think about Tellin. Then I just looked at the stars on the roof again.

They always said in school that the galaxy is so big that humans would never be able to get their heads around it even if they tried to. I think that's true when loads of bad things 'appen too. You get numb after a while and it gets so big you can't get ewer head around it. In the end it does a full circle and ewer back in the beginnin'. Clueless, and naked, like the day you were born. Except I wasn't naked tonight, I was in my pyjamas.

Chapter 12

I slept like a baby that night and Tellin and I met in my dream. I don' feel so angry towards him now. He kissed me and then I woke up. Wakin' up can be so shit sometimes.

When I got out of bed I remembered that Gareth had gone to the mental institute place and I remembered then that Tomtom was dead in a shoebox in the pantry. I was goin' to give him a good funeral. For Nanna. I invited Mam but she ignored me. I had a last look in the shoe box before I put Tomtom deep in the earth and he looked peaceful. His eyes were still open and his little whiskers made him look like he was still alive. That-man-Terry said he wouldn't mind comin' over to help with the diggin'. And I didn't say no. You'd 'ave to be a right dupper to refuse help just because you don't like someone. I brought the little pink ball that Tomtom used to play with and put it in the shoebox. The ball was half flat and I felt exactly like that bloody ball.

I chucked earth all over the shoebox. Clarks box it was. Don't know where the fuck it had come from, mind. Mam never buys shoes from Clarks. Much too dear. Anyhow, I said a prayer for Tomtom, and I said it loud. I said somethin' like, 'I'm sorry you had to be caught in the middle and that the last thing you ever saw was a bowl of custard thrown against a wall.' I said he should go and see Nanna in the nefoedd ('cos that's where she is, in the Welsh side) and I could nearly hear Tomtom purrin'. In fact, I was sure that I heard him purrin'. It was actually my phone buzzin' in my pocket. Shit, I thought. I should have turned it off. Respect and all that. I ignored the phone and I put a flower in a pot on top of the heap of earth. The flower was pink, pretty. Not

Tomtom's colours mind. He was more of a blue. But tough shit really.

I looked at my phone to see who had phoned: I'd had a missed call from Dad. I thought I best call him back to see what he wanted. So I did. He was all quiet, breathin' slow and he said:

'I'm goin' over to see Gareth, in the 'ospital place, fancy comin'?'

I said no, straight away. I knew it might push me over the edge. I could imagine Gareth in a straight jacket, drugged up. Like in the films. I knew it probably wasn't that bad, mind, but I bloody hated 'ospitals and I didn't want to take the risk. Hospitals always made me feel like I was goin' to die. 'Specially these days, with death runnin' after me like a Banshee. I had the guilties after sayin' no because Dad would 'ave to go on his own. But I didn't change my mind.

That afternoon was quiet. But that was alright. Quiet means there's no more to deal with for the time bein'. Mam and Terry went up the Brecon Beacons walkin'. Gentle walkin' mind, that's what Mam said. Because of the baby. Shit, I'd nearly forgotten about all that.

I decided to get out of the house too and the only place I could think about goin' was Anti Peg's house. Dad wouldn't be there because he was goin' to see Gareth and maybe Peg wouldn't mind the company. I jumped on the bus, thinkin' she might cheer me up with her swearin'. There's nothin' better than swearin' sometimes.

As I was standin' and waitin' for the bus to come, I could feel the drizzle in my hair. The last time I was on a bus was when I came back from not meetin' Tellin the night before. Suddenly, I felt like a loser and it felt like years ago when I had actually believed that he was for real. That he actually

127

liked me. That somebody actually liked me. What a bastard, I thought again. If I could get my hands on him now, I'd spit on 'im. How did he manage to make me think he liked me so much? Wanker.

I stood waitin' for the bus a while and I even saw the Welsh Poshos up the street pass. They were all one big 'appy family in a big estate car and they waved through the window. Oh fuck, I thought, they're gonna stop, wind down the window, say hello. But thank God, they didn't. They just carried on drivin'. And I could tell they were goin' on a nice Sunday trip. And that's when I realised it was Sunday. Sunday used to feel special, or different anyway. Now, it meant jack shit and I could still get on a bus to see Anti Peg, like any other day. I used to feel a 'Sunday lunch and gravy' feelin' to Sunday, but ever since Gareth went to Iraq and Dad got locked up, we haven't done anythin' like that in our 'ouse really. And now Sunday's just like any other day.

Finally, at last, the bus came. It took twenty minutes before I reached Anti Peg's house. By the time I'd gotten there, I couldn't be bothered to go in and see her. Awful how things like that 'appen innit? Full of good intention, then all of a sudden, you can't be bloody arsed. Anyway, I knocked on the door and Peg answered straight, as if she was waitin' for me.

'For fuck's sakes get in will you. There's a draft comin' in while you stand about like a fool.'

I knew that I wanted to ask her a bit more about Danny Bishop but I didn't 'ave the guts. Not for now anyhow. I walked through her house and smelled her smell. A weird combination of roses, gravy and dog. And that would make sense, because Anti Peg's got Flo, and Flo's by her side all the time. He's black as soot and he smells like shit. He's really friendly and everythin' but I hate it when dogs jump. And Flo does. Peg says she called Flo 'Flo' after 'Flo me la'. I don't know what the fuck she's on about to be honest, but I just nod. She made me some bara brith and she put butter on it. I hate butter on bara brith, but I didn't say anythin'. I ate it, and it was nice. I ate it quickly and I downed some tea. But as I ate my second piece of bara brith, I nearly spewed. A piece of dog hair was lyin' in the butter. Black and cheeky. Black and long and, fuck, I was sure I had half of it in my mouth, between my teeth. And what did I do at that moment? I spewed, didn't I. Right there, in Peg's front room with pictures of Mam and Dad's weddin' and Nanna, Gramps, Peg and Alf in Porthcawl, all starin' at me from the walls. I was about to ask her about Danny Bishop too. But no, I didn't get a chance did I. Because I spewed. I didn't tell her why I'd spewed. I just said, I'm sorry Peg, I'm sorry Peg. Now, any other old woman would've said, 'Don't you worry, darlin', it's not your fault'. But not Anti Peg. She just said, under her breath,

    'Christ, that's absolutely disgustin'. And it's a new friggin' carpet too.' I still didn't say a thing, mind, about the dog hair. I just sat there breathin'. Then I went to the bathroom, and gargled so that all the spew disappeared. I looked at myself in the mirror and felt like shit. After a bit, I opened the mirrored cupboard for a quick nose. Inside, there were treasures. Bottles, old bottles. Hair colour. Dark hair colour. Facial hair bleach. Tweezers. Fair enough. Shampoo that looked like it should be in Sain Ffagan with dust on the caps, and old crusty soap. And then, out of the corner of my eye, I saw it. Fuck me, I closed the door quickly. I couldn't quite believe it. There, sittin' like a queen amongst them all, was a big purple vibrator. I choked and spewed again, retching into the sink. After that, I raised my head and found that I was sweatin' like a mule. My forehead was wet. I was sickened. But I also felt quite proud of Peg. Good for her, I thought. But fuck me, was she crazy.

Later we settled down to watch the telly on the sofa. Right as rain. I'd managed to push the image of Peg with a shakin' vibrator to the back of my head and I was back with the old Anti I knew. I started watchin' some programme about buildin' houses and Peg looked through the local paper. After a few minutes of readin' it, she tutted. I carried on watchin' the programme. This man from London wanted to buy land in Carmarthen and build a house. Lucky bastard, I thought. Some people have got more money than sense. I wouldn't even be able to rent a flat let alone build a second home. I carried on tryin' to watch the programme, but Peg was makin' a noise. Tuttin' and tuttin'. I think she was readin' somethin' sad.

'T-t-t-tut. Duw, Duw.'

And I didn't ask what was wrong. I couldn't be bothered to be honest. She does that kind of thing quite a lot. I raised my head, but I didn't look at her, I looked over her shoulder. I noticed Dad's clothes folded on a chair by the table on the other side of the room, behind her. All folded tidy. No way did Dad do that, I thought. She's been doin' everythin' for him, I could tell. Washin' his clothes, makin' his food. Anti Peg kept on tuttin'.

'T-t-tut. And such a young one too.'

'What are you on, Peg?' I actually had to ask because she was gettin' on my tits now.

'A young boy love, killed down Porth way on Thursday. Pity.'

'Aye, pity,' I said.

'Walked out in front of a car, without noticin'.'

'Duw,' I said. She was gettin' on my wick now.

'Duw, and he was a pretty boy too. Real green eyes.'

130

I stopped breathin'. I snatched the paper from her paper-thin skin.

'What the fuck are you doin' love?'

I searched the page and saw his face. Clear as day. Oh my life. Oh, my life. It was Tellin. I couldn't believe it. It was him. I felt sick and I wanted to cry and I wanted to smile too, which is really sick. I know it is. It was him, it was Tellin. Shit. My face burned up and Peg just looked at me.

'You knew 'im did you love?'

I didn't say nothin'. I was still sad and glad. Half of me was so sad I could've spewed my insides out and half of me felt, ha, I knew he would've come to meet me if he could have. If he was alive. His picture was huge in the paper. His picture, and a picture of her too. Vicky. She was quite pretty, I suppose. But I didn't look at her photo for long, I just looked at his. At his green, green eyes. I didn't cry mind, I just sat there readin' the article about him, his green eyes shinin' out from the page. Tellin, love, I thought. My God.

The article was the most weird thing I've ever read. It was so different to everythin' I thought I knew. His name was Andrew, Andrew Johns. That felt weird to start. Then I read he 'ad a fiancée. Vicky. That didn't make sense mind. Vicky. He did like me, definite. I felt like I was in a dream. Vicky. No, this was like a nightmare with Anti Peg breathin' down my neck. Andrew, I thought, that felt so weird. And Vicky. Andrew and Vicky. Andrew written in dapper print, underneath Tellin's face. Andrew. Fiancée. Andrew. He went to Rhydfelen school, that's what the piece said. Spoke Welsh then, I thought. We would've had kids who spoke Welsh. Nanna would've loved him. Fuck, I thought, this is crazy, they're both dead and I'm makin' all these things up about him. Open funeral. Andrew. Fiancée. Funeral next week. His

Mam and Dad live in Porth. Visitin' them after a shift. Shit. Andrew. And those green eyes.

I threw the paper to the floor and just sat back and watched the shit programme about buyin' houses. I tried not to think about the death I had just seen. And I couldn't help but feel that the grim reaper also followed anyone who had anythin' to do with my life too. I felt guilty, responsible. Like the kiss of death. Somethin' was bleedin' inside me but the sense in me said, what the fuck are you doin'? You can't mourn someone you never knew. I felt all cold and I couldn't think straight. My ckeeks were red, red. Boilin' they were. But I kept on watchin' the programme about buildin' houses. Anti Peg didn't ask more questions, fair play to her. She was alright really. She just picked the paper up and scrambled her way through the pages until she found the obits. That's all she's really interested in. All the people her age are there now. They're not really in the other bits of the paper. She didn't say she was flickin' to the obits, mind. She knew that wouldn't be right. But that's what she was doin', poppin' her head from the paper every now and then to see if I was alright.

And all I could see was his face. And those green eyes, closed in a coffin, somewhere.

I left Peg to it after a bit. I just wanted to get 'ome. And 'sides, Flo had just done a huge poo by the mantlepiece so I felt sick again. Anti Peg looked a bit embarrassed and then she kissed Flo on the head. She kissed me ta-ta straight after too. Scum. I had loads I wanted to say to her, loads. Loads to ask her too. About Nanna and Danny Bishop. But things had happened now, things had changed everythin'. Tellin was gone.

Mam and that-man-Terry were sharin' a macca pizza when I arrived home. Mam turned to me with rosy cheeks and asked,

'What's wrong love? You look white as a ghost.'

'Jus' a bit cold tha's all.' I didn't 'ave the right to be upset and I never told another soul about seein' Tellin in the paper. Mam wouldn't have understood, I think she'd think I was nuts. I only met him once. Once. She would definitely think I was mental. And she had a son in a mental institute already. But Anti Peg knew, and in a weird way that was enough. I'd gotten the feelin' she'd understood me for a moment.

Anyway, for the rest of that Sunday night I just sat with Mam and Terry in the telly room. I hope they didn't mind. They said they'd enjoyed up the Beacons. I said, cool. I don't think they did. I could see more wrinkles under Mam's eyes than usual but she was still smilin' 'spite the fact she was cryin' inside. For Gareth. And I did the same, I just smiled. Fair play to that-man-Terry. He popped up the shops and got us both a Mars bar each and a pack of fags for himself. We sat there watchin' some film on the telly and I fell asleep. I woke up leanin' on his shoulder, dribblin' too. I felt so embarassed. Mam and Terry laughed and I made my excuses and went upstairs. I had a hollow feelin' in my stomach. Hungry like I've never felt hungry, but I didn't want to eat. I couldn't believe that the love of my life was dead. I felt heartbroken and I felt as if I had no right to feel like that at the same time.

Mixed up as I was, I knew one thing at least: death wasn't scary anymore. Nanna was there, and now Tellin was there too. In the nefoedd. People I loved were there. I'd had this idea recently that in a way life was just like death. Another reality maybe, but just as normal. No, it didn't freak me out that Tellin was dead. It just made me feel as good as dead myself.

Chapter 13

Today I went to the funeral. I don't want anyone thinkin' I'm mental or nothin', but I went. It said 'Open Funeral, Thursday' in the paper so I went. I was half expectin' for there to be loads of young girls like me there – maybe Tellin 'ad been a bit of a player. A row of us, like twats, standin' in the back. Like a bunch of slags. Desperate slags. Turns out it wasn't like that at all.

I took a day off work. Christ, I bet they think I'm preggers or somethin', I'm never there anymore. I wouldn't be surprised if they sack me, after everythin' . . . Anyway, I didn't care what they thought really. This was much more important, so I went.

All the papers and the people had been talkin' about him. That poor young boy, his poor fiancée. All that stuff. His poor fiancée? What about me?

I found the church OK although I didn't think I would. It wasn't far from our house really, just down a street I never go. Funny that, It's been there all my life, closer to my house than my school was and I never knew anythin' about the fuckin' place. Shows you that you don't know as much as you think about where you live. You grow up in this place, and you think you know it like the back of your hand. But you fuckin' don't.

When I got there, I just went straight in and stood at the back. There was a gap between me and all the people in the front, and I was 'appy about that really. I mean, it felt a bit freaky really, bein' there at all. I stood there, with the organ music playin'. No one looked back at me. I could see his Mam and his Dad too. I guessed it was them because they looked well upset. Then, I turned my head and saw this girl lookin' back at me. I looked at her for ages, thinkin' – fuck, don't she work in Custards? She's awful familiar. Then I remembered, it was the girl in the other photo, in the paper. The fiancée. It was Vicky. She looked at me confused, didn't know who I was. Whispered to her mother. She looked back, smiled. I just put my head down. I fetched a tissue from my pocket. Looked at it a while and thought about Gareth. I couldn't believe they said he was good enough to come home now. How could that be? Mam had gone mental when she'd found out. Said that it was awful they didn't give 'im the care he deserved. Said she couldn't believe they couldn't see he needed more help. I think she's just shittin' herself about seein' 'im come 'ome. Scared of 'im even. I don't know. That's unfair. I don't think she is really, but I wouldn't blame her if she was scared. That-man-Terry said that Gareth should live with Peg like he did before, but I think Mam feels guilty 'bout it. She is ancient after all, she might pop her clogs if she has any more excitement in that house. And the thing is, he should be home with us. I couldn't help but feel that that-man-Terry couldn't be bothered with the idea of Gareth comin' back to our house and makin' things awkward for him.

The funeral was weird. I was feelin' really stupid for bein' there when the priest started talkin'. It was like all distant. Like as if he didn't really know Tellin. He was so bad that I felt that I could've done a better job, just from readin' all the stuff in the papers about him. What was it about these preacher men? They didn't seem to know or care who they were talkin' about. And this was someone's funeral. Well, not someone. Not just anyone. This was Tellin's funeral.

Anyway, we stood to sing, which I bloody hate doin' and then everyone went to the graveside. I couldn't help but follow. As we walked, I popped a Tune in my mouth 'cos I had a real sore throat. I really like Tunes, they cheer me up. Better still I love the fact that if you eat too many of 'em it makes you have the shits. Brilliant if you 'aven't been for days. Anyway, I followed and I just hoped that no one noticed me. It could have gone smoothly, with people just assumin' that I was with someone else. I tried not to draw attention to myself but I could see that Vicky girl lookin' back sometimes – and I just thought, bloody get lost. Just because you don't know who I am doesn't mean you can stare at me. As we stopped by the hole where Tellin would be lowered into, she stared some more. I wanted to shout, 'What's wrong? Gorra telly on my 'ead or wha'?' but I didn't. I couldn't really, could I? Not in a funeral. Not in Tellin's funeral. Not in her fiancée's funeral. And anyway, I had more important things to do. I had one more thing I really wanted to do, to say 'thank you' to Tellin. After all, he did save my life.

We all stood in a circle and the priest said a prayer. I felt awful sad for his parents and his brother. His brother lived in Australia, but he had come back. All brown and blonde haired. I stood behind everyone, right in the back. But this old woman kept draggin' me closer and I felt as if I was a part of this circle. The Vicky girl scowled at me. Hated me.

I know it's a weird thing to think, but I couldn't quite believe that the body of the only person I've ever thought was lush was in the wooden box by where we were standin'. I wondered for a while whether he was watchin' this funeral. But I guessed that he was probably too busy, sortin' things out up there. After all, he'd only just arrived. I felt a bit shit that I was in the funeral of a person that maybe, wouldn't have wanted me to be there at all. But it wasn't as if he had a choice who could come to his funeral. No one has that choice.

And I suppose that's a really good point actually, your funeral is so out of your control. That's ever so funny isn't it? I mean, you go through your life invitin' the people you want to your parties, or to your weddin', makin' sure some idiots don't come and then when the most important date comes along you're not around to say who can't come. Maybe my funeral will be packed full of randoms or twats I don't like. Oh my life. Oh *my* life.

They lowered the coffin and everyone cried. I just stood there, feelin' more awkward than ever before. I didn't cry. The feelin' I had was so sad and hollow, I couldn't have cried even if I tried. I felt the thing in my pocket, the thing I had bought. It's nearly time, I thought.

I forgot thinkin' 'orrible thoughts when everyone started throwin' nice things on his coffin. Some threw flowers, some earth, a teddy bear, a rugby ball, a catalogue. A fuckin' catalogue! No one better throw in a tin of custard when I die I thought. I knelt towards the coffin and threw my special thing in. I prayed quick and quiet, saying 'Thank you for savin' my life'. I wanted it all to be over then, no more drama, no fuss. No one to notice, no one to give a shit. But, when I lifted my head, all hell broke loose. Vicky was standin' right by me.

'Look! I knew she was a freak!'

Older women came and held her. 'What's wrong bach? Calm down.'

'She's fuckin' thrown somethin' weird in on the coffin,' she spat before looking over at me. She brushed her hair behind her ears as if she was preparin' for a fight. An oldish man came up to me after that, lookin' me up and down.

'If ew don' mind me askin' love, who the fuck are you?'

'No one,' I said. He looked towards the coffin and held my arm.

'Why in God's name have you thrown a fish finger down there then?'

I cringed. How do you explain somethin' like this? I looked up at everyone.

'Christ! She's mental,' said the Vicky girl again. The priest looked at her angry because she'd used the Lord's name in vain.

'Give the girl a few moments,' said the priest. I breathed.

'Tellin, Andrew, he saved my life once.'

Everyone looked at me funny. Then, with no messin', Vicky jumped towards me and pulled my hair.

'You shagged 'im, it's obvious. I can tell it in your eyes.'

I wish, I thought, but I never said a thing. I just got dragged by the hair. Soon I was on the floor. Everyone tried to stop her but she managed to kick me. I could see her tits because her black top was movin' all over the shop while she clambered on the floor. They were bigger than mine. Miles.

I fell back, more in shock than pain. I fell back – but didn't land on the floor. I tried to fall flat on my back on the floor but that just didn't happen. I tried, I really did try. Although I tried not to, half my body fell into the hole in the ground and I rolly-pollied back, out of control, onto Tellin's coffin. I'd been buried alive. Gasps, I could hear gasps. Cryin' too. Then everythin' jus' went black.

About an hour later, or so I was told, I woke up, in a really soft pink bed. I was absolutely gutted and really confused. Was this heaven? Hardly. Not with wallpaper like that. I looked around and could see that a woman was sittin' in the corner, cryin' with a crumpled-up, half-wet tissue. She looked up and noticed that I had opened my eyes. She ran over to my side. Who the fuck was this?

'You alright, love?'

'Yeah, thank-you.'

'For a moment there, we thought we'd 'ave to take you to 'ospital.'

'Did you?'

'Yes love, you could've easliy died. Knocked ewer 'ead. Andrew would've . . .'

She cried again and I felt like a twat. I shouldn't 'ave fuckin' gone.

'Sorry.'

'Nothin' for you to be sorry for. It's that slapper's fault. Vicky. I always wanted Andrew to move on, but he was too nice a boy.'

Fuck me, it was his mother, I thought. Turns out I was wrong. She was actually Andrew's mother's sister. His Anti then. She was really nice to me, and she didn't need to be. I think she was intrigued, wanted to know who the fuck I was and what the fuck I was doin' in her nephew's funeral.

In a really twisted way I felt as if I had done this deliberate, to meet the family. But, I knew I hadn't. At least, I didn't think I had . . .

'Marlene wants to know how you knew 'im.'

Marlene, his Mum. Must be.

'I didn't really.'

'Oh,' she said, a little disappointed.

'She thinks you looked his type.'

'His type?'

'Oh, don't worry love.'

I felt like a fool again, I had to say somethin', how I knew 'im, or else, why the hell was I at the funeral? Did I just crash these things for fun?

'Well, he saved my life once.'

'Aye, we all heard you say that. But Marlene thought it was a lie. Said that no way that was the truth, because of what you threw in the coffin and all.'

'A fish finger . . .?' I sort of asked, because lookin' back, it was the stupidest thing I've ever done. How did I think I'd be able to justify that?

'Aye,' she said, 'there was defo somethin' fishy about that.'

I tried not to laugh, she obviously hadn't clicked about what she had just said.

'He worked sellin' catalogues?'

'Aye', she looked at me, intrigued. She didn't have a clue where this was goin'. I knew she thought, you bloody well know a lot more about him than you're lettin' on. And the truth was, I didn't. Although I thought I did.

'I answered the door once, thought it was my Dad . . .'

'Right . . .' She said, leanin' forward. She was expectin' Mills and Boon, I could tell. She held her tissue tight, except it didn't even look like a tissue anymore.

'But it was him, and I choked, on a . . .'

She smiled, 'Fish finger?' Look at Miss Marple here . . .

'Aye, and he, knocked it out my throat,' I sat up in the soft bed, and I got a bit dizzy.

'Good God, that was somethin' fishy then, wasn't it!'

I looked at her again.

'Aye.'

She was laughin', 'Do you get it? Fishy. Get it? Fishy! Fish fingers!' Got it the first time you daft cow, I thought. I smiled. 'Marlene wants to meet you.'

'No,' I said quickly. I answered automatic pilot. It made me feel sick, weird.

'She wants to know about all this . . .'

'But that's it, I've said all there is to say now see. I saw him in the paper, that's all. I saw the news about, about this, all this, in the paper.'

'Aye, maybe, but she'd still like to know,' she touched my shoulder. 'I think it would make it easier for her you know.'

I put my head back on the pillow. How could I have gotten myself into such a mess? For fuck's sakes! And now I was gettin' blackmailed into meetin' his mother.

'I'll pop down to get her.'

I sat up, thought it out. I couldn't do it. I felt sick. My God. No way, I'd feel like a stalker. I sat up in bed, felt a bit dizzy, but I still did. Then I grabbed my clothes. Pulled my legs from bed. Felt naked in a stranger's house. Was this Tellin's house? I felt mental, so I dressed and I stood up, and I ran. I ran and ran through shit loads of people, in black, down the stairs. Out through the back door and ran. I ran, ran, ran. That Vicky girl saw me escape and ran after me. She couldn't catch up with me mind. Not that I'm fit, but she was a bit fat, and the fact of the matter was she was runnin' with a ham sandwich on white in one hand and a fag in the other. I felt like I was in a chase in a film. Like that boy in *Weddin' Crashers*. But I was the hero in the film, I was the one that was goin' to get away. Even if I had to jump over a huge fence . . . well, maybe.

When I got 'ome, all swollen and puffed out, I just tried to forget it all. My brain couldn't catch up with itself. I sat on the sofa for about ten minutes. I tried to act normal, forget what had just taken place. Don't think about it, I thought. I felt faint and really thirsty but I just stared at the telly. I sat there for half an hour without even noticin' that Gareth was there too. A full half hour!

'Jesus, Gareth! I didn't see you. Why 'aven't you said hello?'

'Thought you was ignorin' me.'

'Ignorin' you? How could I have ignored you if I didn't know you were there?'

'Like you just did.'

'Why the fuck would I do that?'

'Didn't want to make a fuss. Thought perhaps you was mad about the cat.'

'Well,' I said.

Then we just sat in silence. It was obvious Gareth was on calmin' drugs, but to be honest, I was fuckin' glad. We sat there watchin' repeats of old *Who Wants To Be a Millionaire?*. He looked younger. Like a different Gareth. He didn't freak me out, because he's always been different to me. And truth be told, I was mad about Tomtom. I hated the idea that he had killed the cat in a rage. It made me feel angry myself. I reckon Gareth was thinkin' the same as me as we sat there. Thank the Lord no one is sayin' nothin' then. Sometimes quiet is exactly what you need.

I remember when Mam, Dad, me and him used to watch 'Who Wants to be a Millionaire?' when it started. And I remember how Chris Tarrant used to look sorted, instead of bein' fucked up and lonely like he is now. It was the best thing since sliced bread it was. Everyone loved it, Dad even tried to get on it. He gave up after a while though. Not because he didn't think he could answer the questions. He reckoned he could still do that. The main thing was he got the difficult questions right a lot of the time but the ones at the start caught him out. Weird that. But anyway, that was years ago now.

I went to bed that night thinkin' nothin' about the funeral. I didn't let myself. I put Classic FM on and pretended to be on a lilo on the sea. I tried to sleep quickly but that just didn't happen. I floated in and out of Classic FM and my own random thoughts. I thought about sharks and colourful fish underneath the lilo, all goin' about doin' their own thing, not hurtin' no-one. Little did I know that a fish finger was soon goin' to swim under the lilo too. A little teeny-tiny fish finger. I remember watchin' some documentary once where they showed how a butterfly's wings can create a hurricane in another part of the world. In fish terms, I knew that this teeny-tiny fish finger was about to create a big wave too. A wave like a six-foot wall.

Chapter 14

Today was random. Actually, it was possibly the most random day of my whole random life. I woke up after dreamin' that I was gonna be some kind of funeral director when I was grown up. I mean, when I'm about thirty or somethin'. Maybe it was because I couldn't sleep last night and while I was sleepin' (or tryin' to sleep), there was a weird programme on Classic FM. It can be quite a cool programme sometimes but last night's was weird. It's like a kind of listeners' hour when all fucked-up people (as in, people who 'ave had to go through fucked-up things) get a chance to ask for their favourite pieces of classical music. One old man once asked for a Mozart piece because he 'ad only just lost his dog and when he played Mozart in the house he could hear the dog scramblin' about upstairs, howlin' although he was as dead as a dodo. It was fuckin' obvious who was howlin' if ew ask me.

Anyway, last night's one was about this girl who had lost her older sister. Bless her. It sounded 'orrible and I felt awful lucky that everyone ('cept for Nanna and Tellin) was alive. Anyway, the sister that was still alive started sayin' that she got her sister's ashes and gave them to a company who turned 'em into a diamond. Now, I 'aven't got the fuckin' faintest idea how someone does that, but she did it. And then, and this is the fucked-up part if ew ask me, she got the diamond put in her tooth. So she carried her sister around in her mouth. Just imagine that. Only, the tragedy was that she woke up one mornin' and it 'ad gone. She'd only gone and swallowed 'er own fuckin' sister. Jock Fieldin', the DJ, said he was awful sorry to hear such a story and they played some kind of mini-wet or somethin' for her. I wanted to hear the song, but I fell asleep.

Then, I suppose there's no surprise really – that I dreamed of bein' this weird funeral director. Loads of people phoned me and asked me for random requests – can you send my father's ashes through the post? Can you scatter my dog's ashes on my car? Can you pop my ashes in a milk tray box and scatter them all over the Tesco car park up Newport way? Someone even asked me to arrange a funeral in a public toilet. I seriously didn't understand that. I must be really fucked up in my head. But anyway, it was only a dream, so I forgot about it. And to be honest, it was nice to be able to remember bits of the dream as I woke up and poked my fingers into my eyes, tryin' to get rid of the cwsg. It let me forget about my real life for a bit, forget about the funeral yesterday, forget how much of a tit I'd been. I kept on feelin' really confused. How the fuck did I end up in his house? I was about to force myself to go back to bed when someone knocked on my bedroom door.

It was Mam, she looked a bit pissed off and excited too.

'A boy called Brandon on the phone, says he's from the *Ponty Observer*.'

'What?', I said in a really croaky voice. 'Can ew take a message? I gorra get to work see.'

I was sure it was the wrong number. No one like that ever phoned me. Fuck, I thought. I had a really scary feelin' that it was about the signs I'd written wrong on the lorries in Welsh. I started sweatin'.

'Oh, I don't think it's nothin' to worry 'bout, love,' she smiled.

'No, but what the fuck does he want? Somethin' to do with Custards?' I felt panicky, as if the paparazzi were outside my door. Ready to expose me.

'Mind ewer language.'

'Sorry Mam.'

145

'He said somethin' about a . . . fish finger?'

I looked up at her. She smiled. I wanted to cry.

'Well hurry up then, you silly cow, he's on the phone waitin'.'

I ran from the room, down the stairs. Shit. This was a mess. What the hell 'ad they been up to?

'Hello?'

'Samantha?'

'Aye', I tried to swallow but I couldn't.

'I'm phonin' because of the incident with the young man, savin' you? Do you remember? The young man who passed away?'

'Right,' I sounded so quiet that I gave him the wrong impression, big style.

'You did know did you? That Andrew Johns 'ad passed away?'

'Um, yeah, I knew, but I didn't know 'im really see.'

'But you were in the funeral?'

'Um, aye, payin' my respects. Sayin' thank you innit.'

Mam came to stand by the phone. She was doin' the 'eye' thing. The 'what's he sayin' then love?' type look. Not knowin' whether to smile or not. I looked at her and did the 'fuck off will ew, Christ can't someone 'ave a few minutes to herself anymore?' thing with my hand. She still stood there, and that-man-Terry came over soon afterwards. I tried to be cryptic.

'So Sam, is it OK if I call you Sam?'

'Aye, go ahead.'

'Great, Sam, well the *Ponty Observer* would like to, well, do a spread on the story you know. Local girl saved, by a young man who's recently passed away . . .?'

'Oh right?'

Mam and that-man-Terry came closer.

'I'm sorry, is this upsettin' for you?'

'Um, no, ummh, I don't know really. Ummh, I mean, well . . .'

Then he went for the kill.

'See, 'is family got in touch about it. Couldn't believe that Andrew was a local hero, and that he didn't say a thing.'

Emotional blackmail I thought. And I hated people callin' him Andrew, 'stead of Tellin. Oh my God, I thought, what a friggin' mess. I had no choice.

'Fine, yeah, 'course.'

'Great, cheers Sam. I'll send a photographer out in about an hour, then I'll pop round later tonight. Where will you be about 9 ish this mornin'? I'll be able to tell Arthur then see, to get ewer photo.'

'Ummh, well, work. Ummh, Custards, up the cwm, the, the . . . Ummh, that's fine.'

'Great stuff, top banana. And I'll come by ewer place tonight for the interview alright love?'

Top banana? I hadn't 'eard that for bloody years. He must've been a lot older than me, but still thought he was young. I put the phone down after sayin' bye and ran upstairs.

'Well?!' shouted Mam from the porch.

'Somethin' to do with Custards, wants to take a picture of us all in work, for somethin' about factories.'

'Oh right,' said Mam, a bit disappointed soundin'.

When I got into the car park in Custards, I could see him sittin' there, in his car. He was there already. I had hoped nothin' would come of it, that it was all a bad dream. But he was there, sittin' in his escort, and he 'ad a beard, and looked too bored to be alive. He saw me and jumped from the car. He had a bag holdin' his camera (presumably) and a box of fish fingers in the other. Oh my God, I thought. I told him I

147

had to go check with my boss if it was alright for me to 'ave the photo, and that I'd be back.

I went straight to Chief's office. Knocked. Went in. He was sittin' there, surfin' the internet. Those stupid naked women were both up this time, on the either side of his head. And now there were two posters advertisin' Death of The Sales, Man! gigs.

'Well, fuck me. Ewer Majesty is gracin' us with her presence.'

'I know, I'm sorry. It's been a funny time. Sorry about Friday, I 'ad a funeral.'

I knew that would give 'im the guilties. And I was also quite disappointed that he'd sworn to my face. After all, he was my sort of boss.

'Aye, aye love. We know, you've 'ad a rough time of it. What d'you want? Somethin' 'bout ewer Mam again?'

I smiled sarcastically. He smiled back, thought he was fuckin' hilarious.

'No, not quite.'

'What then? Quick. I got a team meetin' in two . . .'

'Ummh, can I take ten minutes? There's someone come to take my picture see.'

'Take ten minutes? Take ewer picture? It bloody is Her Royal Highness, Duchess of Porth.'

'It's a long story, cringe too.'

'Fine, just make sure you get Custards in the background right? Now bugger off!'

I smiled and thanked him with my eyes. I didn't want to be too much of a suck. I went outside and old Mr Moody was waitin' for me. He 'ad a cockney accent, real ugly soundin' and he popped a fish finger in my hand.

'Turn a bit,' he said, 'a bit more . . . hold the fish finger up . . . up . . . there you go. And stay there . . . One more . . .

OK . . . don't smile . . . OK . . . and . . . great, thanks. Do you want to keep that fish finger?' I looked at 'im as if he 'ad gone mental. 'Fair enough. Now you know what a lonely old man's avin' for his suppa.'

Get over yourself, I thought. I smiled and walked away. But, I heard 'im again.

'Uh, uh, uh! 'Ang on a minute. Details,' he scrambled his way through the leather camera bag. 'I'll need all your details, what's this place called? – and all that.'

I popped all the details down on a pad of paper he found, and went. Cringe, I thought, all the staff were lookin' through the window at me. Some smiled and some thought, who the fuck does she think she is, Victoria Beckham? I could tell.

Nothin' 'appened in work. Nothin' at all. Maggie was there. She tried to get it out of me about the 'date' I'd supposedly been on last week but I just did the nose thing with my finger. My business, not yours – type thing. Loads of people kept askin' me about me havin' my photo taken, but I didn't say nothin' much. I just told 'em it would all be in the paper soon, because it would.

I dreaded the thought of goin' back home. I knew the bloody Brandon man from the Observer was goin' to be there, and Mam would know everythin'. She was workin' nights this week. I hated the idea that everythin' that had been goin' on in my head was common knowledge to everyone. It was a nightmare. As I walked home I texted Arse. 'Have I got stories for you . . . Caru tx'. Funny how we still say some Welsh words. More for a laugh really. I felt I had to text her, before she saw my name in the Observer. I felt I had to have one person who could hear the whole thing from my side. Although, I was pretty sure that Tellin was watchin' and followin' everythin' from a distance too.

Chapter 15

What can I say? When I got back to the house that-man-Terry and Mam were talkin' to that Brandon from the paper. When I walked into the telly room, they all just looked up at me.

'Oh, love,' said Mam with tears in her eyes, 'Why in fuck's name 'aven't you told us all this?'

'All wha'?', I asked, hopin' they were talkin' about somethin' else.

'How he picked ew up from the floor, did mouth to mouth, pulled the fish finger out, chucked it in the bush outside and then told ew, you were beautiful . . .', Mam looked at me all dewy eyed.

'Now, 'ang on a minute here,' I said and looked at Brandon. Who 'ad been fibbin'? Someone 'ad been makin' things up, bein' an arsehole. It was 'im wasn't it, that journalist bloke. He wants a better story, fuck me, I was mad. Tampin' in fact.

'Now, now Sam,' said the Brandon bloke. It was weird to see his face after imaginin' him for a whole day. He 'ad an 'orrible thin moustache on his face, and I know he thought it looked cool. But he didn't look cool, he looked pants. 'I know it must be 'ard that everyone knows everythin' now, of 'ow he carried you into the house and . . .'

'. . . Carried me into the house?' I looked at him mental. There was somethin' really ugly about the man. Mulin' even. He had one tooth that pointed out further than the rest.

'Andrew's Mam 'as said everythin' Sam, you told her after the funeral and . . .'

I couldn't believe this, I didn't have a choice now. I was sure I hadn't said anythin' like that after the funeral, but I

150

couldn't be sure. And I hadn't even met his Mam anyway! But it was all lies, bollocks, anyway. At least I thought it was. It sounded like a Hollywood film. Now, I don't know why but I thought quite fast and realised – either Brandon's lyin', Tellin's Mum is lyin' to make her son sound like a bloody George-cross hero or I've made it up when I was semi-concussed after the funeral. But one thing was certain, I didn't have a choice now, I couldn't take it back could I? I'd make a dead boy look like a twat. And that's one thing you're still not allowed to do. Make fun of a dead person. Oh no, no one is allowed to gyp a dead person. If he died young, he was a hero; or if he'd been a girl, he was an angel; and if he or she died old, they were legends or survivors or both. I was fucked. I looked at Mam and felt completely trapped.

And then, I started cryin'. I was sure people like Kylie Minogue and Michael Jackson 'ad felt like this in their lives. Someone had gotten the story completely wrong about them. All lies. But, you'd look like more of a tosser if you protested. I cried and Mam stood up. She gave me a cwtsh.

'Don't you worry bach, it's good you can get it out. It's always better like 'at. To think you've kept this quiet for such a long time.'

It was weird, 'cos for the first time ever I noticed Mam's belly up against mine. It was more swollen, it was full of baby. I could feel it. And weirdly, I went from cryin' about bein' trapped by the paparazzi to cryin' for Tellin. Cryin' that we never 'ad the chance to meet. Cryin', cryin' and cryin' until the skin around my eyes was wet and shiny. Mam held me, but I don't think she realised that my cryin' was so deep. It was still nice to have a cwtsh from Mam though.

Brandon was still scribblin' some crap on a pad of paper. That-man-Terry just sat really awkward on the edge of the sofa. Gareth had come in durin' the cryin'. He'd sat down for two minutes and then stood up, and left the room. Couldn't cope, I reckon.

I sat down after a while and told Brandon 'stuff'. Just what he wanted to hear. He was lovin' it too. Sad bastard. I felt as if the story everyone thought they knew was out there now. I couldn't exactly change it, and make it less dramatic. And in a way, I must admit, it was kind of nice to make the fish finger thing sound like a magic Hollywood moment. Of course, I knew it wasn't. Suddenly, I felt a bit weird. All my life I've been makin' things bigger and more colourful in my head. And now the world agreed with me, it was pissin' me off. I felt like the world was gettin' soppy, fallin' for my stories while I was gettin' older. More sarcastic and more . . . I'm sure there's a word. Cynical.

Anyway, Brandon left and time passed. My English teacher in school used to say somethin' like that. Time runneth through the roughest hour or somethin'. She was goin' through a divorce at the time, mind. And I was goin' through tabloid hell today. But knowin' it would be over some time soon, and that time would carry on regardless, made me feel better.

Of course, it wasn't really over. Next day, I popped into the newsagent before goin' into work. I fancied some Skips for dinner. I love Skips, they just melt on your tongue. And I bloody well deserved 'em after all last week's shit. When I went in, the bell on the door chimed and Emma, who always serves me, was smilin'. Emma was in school with me. Her father owns the shop and an electrical company. Our school always asked her father if he wanted to sponsor different events. Now, I've always reckoned there was this deal made then. Because, all of a sudden, Emma started 'avin' parts in

152

the sioe ysgol. Needless to say, she couldn't sing. She was shit, in fact. Anyway, I didn't have anythin' against her. She was OK. But why was she smilin'? She was three years older than me in school. And at the time that was a big deal. I think it was still a big deal for her now too. I remember she got in shit once because her boyfriend was from the English school next door and he kept comin' into our yard and heavy pettin' with her behind *Gwyddoniaeth*.

'Duw, Duw. I thought I smelled somethin' fishy!' she laughed, puttin' her hand on my hand. You're only three fuckin' years older than me, I thought, get ewer hands off! She smiled again. 'No, no, fair play. It's not a laughin' matter really. Fair play to 'im innit? He sounded like ewer angel. I've gorran angel too you know . . .'

I wasn' listenin' by now. I'd twigged, I'd caught on, like a fish on a line. All I could think about doin' now was fetchin' the damn thing. So, I just ran over to the newspaper stand, grabbed a *Ponty Observer* and started ploughin' my way through it. Emma was just laughin', lookin' at me with her arms folded. It wasn't like she was a bitch but she was enjoyin' the spectacle. I could 'ave friggin' strangled her.

'Oh, no,' she said, 'you won't find it in there,' she giggled. Slag.

'Well where is it then?' My cheeks were red by now. I tried not to sound moody with her, but I think it came out that way.

'Hold ewer horses now. You 'aven't looked at the front yet.'

Oh my . . . Christ . . . fuckin' hell. I couldn't look . . . I couldn't . . . they wouldn't have . . . they wouldn't have done that . . . would they? . . . I wanted to look, but I really didn't. I wanted to, I had to, I wanted to . . . So I did . . .

153

In front of my eyes and my burnin' cheeks was a huge, fat photo. Big and in colour. It was a huge, big fat photo of me on the front page of the *Ponty Observer*. I looked like a twat. I looked fat. I looked mulin', muntin' even. It looked as if my face had been skewed and stretched. It didn't look like me. Did it? It didn't. And above the picture of me holdin' a fish finger outside Custards, (stood all gay and twisted, like I was in a musical), was the headin':

HERO SAVED SAM FROM FISHY END
BEFORE TRAGIC CRASH.

My name, my fishy end. My embarrassin' fishy end. I might 'as well 'ave fuckin' died. I couldn't believe it, and the title was so shit, I could 'ave written somethin' better myself. Then there was this big article, (all full of lies of course) that carried on underneath the picture with 'continued on page 4 . . .' written after it. More of it? More bloody lies? I read the article slowly. As I did, I remembered I was in the newsagent. I turned around and Emma was still starin'. I turned back to the paper and twisted myself so that she couldn't see my face. Thank God, the door chimed and someone else came into the shop. I carried on reading and I saw a quote by Tellin's Mam. It nearly broke my heart.

'Andrew was always so humble. To think he had saved that young girl's life and not said a sausage . . . and carryin' her into the house too. He was ever so strong, everyone said that.'

That's weird, I thought. The fact that she'd said 'not said a sausage' in the quote. It didn't seem right somehow. Not the type of words you'd want to use really. Then there was a quote from his ex-headmaster.

'Though he left school before attaining his GCSEs, Andrew always showed initiative. It came as no surprise to me to hear that he was an avid salesperson and a lifesaver too. He will be sorely missed.'

Left school before doin' his GCSEs, I thought, good God. I wouldn't have thought that. Readin' between the lines, he seemed to have been a right arse-hole in school. One of those boys I would've hated. But he must've sorted himself out, as he did seem nice enough when I met him. At least, he 'ad a spark. And GCSEs can't give you that.

I looked at Emma after readin'. The person who'd come in had gone. I folded the paper tidily and put it back where I'd found it.

'Inew gonna buy tha' then?'

'No,' I said. Coolly and calmly, I walked over to the crisps stand and took a packet of Skips. After all, that's why I'd gone in there. I went to the counter, paid for them and tried not to look as if I was stormin' out. But I did, I stormed out. God give me strength.

The bus stop is directly outside the newsagents and weirdly, when I got out the shop, the bus I needed was there. I jumped on and had that weird feelin' that I was in a film. Everythin' was slick and smooth. A few people looked at me. Had they seen the papers? Or did they always 'ave a quick look at everyone? I sat there, and felt like shit. All paranoid, like a famous person.

As I looked out at the Rhondda through the window, I had time to sit and think. The grey sky was pressin' down on me today. There wasn't any fog, and no rain either, but the sky just pressed down against me. I can't really explain. My ordeal, and my secret affair with Tellin 'ad turned into one big laugh, and I knew it. I knew people were laughin'. And anyway, what they'd read was all lies anyway. They'd made it sound so glam, so dramatic. And although it wasn't me who fed the fire, I felt like a liar, a cheat. And worse than that, everyone knew about Tellin and me and yet they knew fuck all. Because really, there was fuck all to know. I could've been sick that mornin' on the way to work. Serious, I could 'ave. Sick like a dog after chewin' grass.

When I got into Custards, I had the usual lot smilin' and smirkin'. Big Ben said 'Hello' and touched my shoulder. Creep. Ajeet popped his head around the door to my office.

'Media storm abrewing, yes Samantha?', and winked. Oh, get lost. Ajeet was the only person who ever really called me Samantha. Then Percy passed me, but he didn't say a word. His way of sayin' 'I saw you in the paper', if you ask me. And I'm sure some famous person said once, that not bein' talked about is worse than bein' talked about. Oh, I don' know.

I sat down at last, and I was so glad to look at my computer without it speakin' back, or smirkin' at me. Maggie came in then. She'd been to the toilet, and sat down quietly.

'Go on then, you say something too. Everyone else has.'

'Chief and me, we're engaged.'

'No way,' I said lookin' into her eyes. She did look pretty today. A bit tired, but pretty for Maggie. She wasn't smilin' though. I couldn' believe she hadn't said anythin' about the fish. I felt a bit miffed in a way. I was gettin' used to all the attention. But I suppose that was fair enough. She was gettin' engaged. Despite everythin', she was gettin' engaged. Despite all that business with Gareth and all.

'Aye, nuts innit? Anyway, what did you mean, say somethin'?'

'Oh nothin'.' I looked at her again: 'Congrats then.'

I wanted to say to her that all I could think about was

'How come you're gettin' married when you were shaggin' my brother a few weeks ago?' I felt awful hard then, awful cold. Why couldn' I just get over it and be chuffed for her.

'Aye, we're gonna make it soon.'

'God, cool. Why the hurry?'

She looked at me and I knew. She didn't have to say anything. She was pregnant again wasn' she, and I'd been such a shit friend, never around, not readin' any signs. Nothin'. Then suddenly, it dawned on me. She'd only just gotten rid of one baby, and now she was expectin' again. Bloody hell. And then somethin' else dawned on me. Could Gareth be . . .?

'Sorry, I should've, I haven't been . . .'

She stopped me.

'Coffee?'

She never asked me if I wanted a cuppa. We didn't really drink tea nor coffee on our table. Never. I pushed what I'd just thought of to the back of my mind.

'Ummh, OK. But, look, I haven't, you know, been . . .'

'I haven't either,' Maggie coughed, 'I should've been there for you, with everyone, well with all the things that's 'appened to you.'

This was cringin' me out big style. I hated havin' heart to hearts. And the funny thing was, she didn't know the half of what had been goin' on, yet. We decided we'd go for a pastie dinnertime and have a chat. And that's what we did. We didn't say everythin' to each other 'course; I didn't mention Gareth nor nothin', because sometimes it's bad news to tell someone everythin'. You haven't got anythin' left for ewer self then. And the weird thing was, although we were like old friends again, some things had 'appened that meant we would never quite be the same. I think I looked up to Maggie

157

before. But by now I knew she was just a person. Full of black and white.

'Mam's pregnant too,' I said. It didn't mean nothin' to me now. It was neither here nor there. It wasn't as if I'd thought about it a lot but it had sunk in. Things do that over time, even if you haven't thought about them. It's as if your brain, but not your brain, has been sortin' things out for you.

'Fuck off!' Was her answer when she heard Mam was pregnant.

'Aye, she's not that old really see,' I said, takin' a big bite of my corned beef pasty.

She just stared at me.

'No, I spose she isn't. Who's the Dad?'

Stupid question, and I could ask you the same fuckin' thing, I thought.

'That-man-Terry, innit,' I answered a bit short, while chewin'.

'What, they're still together?'

'Aye.' Why would that be such a surprise?

'Does ewer Dad know?'

'No,' I said.

After that, we both walked back and saw Chief on the way. He was standin' by the entrance.

'Well, well, Captain Birdseye! Look at you.'

'Fuck off, Chief,' I said, playfully.

Maggie looked at me, with eyes that said 'Why did you swear? He's ewer boss.' Chief didn't look too impressed either. I hate that. When swearin' in the wrong places makes you look like a twat.

'No, fair play to you, you did mention Custards. I would 'ave fuckin' quartered you if ew adn't.'

'What's he on about?' asked Maggie, when we walked through the doors.

'Nothin' really, take a look at the *Ponty Observer* when ew ger 'ome tonight.' I 'ad to say didn't I?

'Ewer a dark horse you are,' she looked at me, looked me up and down too.

'I think you'll find I'm a dark sea horse actually.'

'Eh?' I saw her fillings.

'Nothin', just read the bloody paper.' We settled down to workin', and that was that.

Gettin' 'ome that night was a relief. I felt like a superstar and so it was nice to get out of the limelight. There were three cards on the table in the kitchen, all with my name on 'em. Mam came from downstairs, she'd been sleepin'. She's workin' nights.

'Alright love? Saw the paper.'

'You and all the world.'

'There's no need to be like that.' She played with her hair and made a tighter knot around her waist with her dressing-gown string. 'I was really proud of you, you know. Everyone is.'

'Why? 'Cos I nearly choked on a fish finger?' My sarcasm was startin' to get on my own nerves. But I never knew how to stop it.

'Look love, things 'ave been 'ard over the last few weeks. With Nanna and with the baby and everythin',' she put her hand, irritatingly, on her belly. 'Terry, Gareth and the fish finger. Tomtom as well.'

I turned away and fetched a mug, 'I 'aven't really thought about it.'

'No love, that's fine, but it's bound to leave a mark, make you mad or somethin'.'

They 'ad come one after another, she was right, but I hadn't thought about it really. 'And ewer Dad too,' she smiled. 'What will we do with ewer Dad?'

I hated that type of talk. She made him sound little, pathetic, sad.

'I'm goin' up there tonight actually.'

'Are you?' she asked, crossin' her eyes.

'Aye, to 'ave supper with Anti Peg and Dad.' Fuck, why did I have to say that? I thought. Lyin' through my teeth.

'Ok, well, if that's what you want.'

I slammed the mug down on the top.

'Yeah, it is what I want, actually. 'Cos I've had it up to fuckin' here with you!' I shouted, lookin' at Mam. Don't get angry, I thought, don't take it out on her. I knew I was doin' it, but I couldn't stop. 'You, you, you! That's all I've heard recently. You bring this man 'ome, next thing ewer 'avin' a baby, and it's you who fucked this family up in the first place. You could've helped Dad through, through . . . everythin'!'

'Sam,' she said. She really didn't 'ave the strength to fight back, I could tell.

'He only fuckin' hit you once, and that was only 'cos you deserved it. You shouldn't 'ave 'ad an affair!'

She looked empty, 'Is that what you think?'

I started cryin' and left. She looked upset, beyond cryin'. I felt so awful, so guilty. I didn't mean what I'd said. I didn't mean a word of it. I wouldn't 'ave been able to cope with Dad, I would've thrown 'im out if I was his wife. I would 'ave fuckin' killed 'im. But for some reason I felt angry. Angry like I 'adn't felt before. And I'd taken it all out on her.

I slammed the front door shut and left for Anti Peg's house. I didn't have a choice. I jumped on the bus, and everythin' reminded me of different things. You know when you're so tired sometimes that you just get this weird feelin' that everyone you see, you know. I saw a person climb on the bus, an old lady. I thought it was Nanna. I thought it was fuckin' Nanna. I felt sick again, thinkin' about all the things I'd said to Mam. I felt bad. I looked through the window and saw a cat. Tomtom I thought. The smell on the bus made me think about Tellin, and Tellin and me and all that love seemed so far away. It seemed further away from my head because everyone seemed to know the story, but that it wasn't the story at all. No one would ever know the real story, and I'd never tell no one either. 'Cos it was all a bit fuckin' mental. Maybe it would be best if I never told Arse about it either. I started feelin' a bit nuts, I got a bit short of breath, worried that I 'ad some illness, that I'd imagined this boy existed when really he didn't. Then I remembered that there were three cards on the table in the kitchen for me. Shit, I'd forgotten to open them.

When I got to Anti Peg's 'ouse, it didn't look as if anyone was home. I knocked the door hard but soon enough Peg answered. I could 'ear her swearin' from outside.

'Oh, for fuck's sakes, who in hell's name would be knockin' now?' She opened the door, smiled. 'Sam darlin', I didn't expect that kind of reception.

'Alright Peg?'

'Aye, now you get in from that damp. It's fuckin' 'orrible outside innit?'

'Aye, where's Dad?' she pushed me through the corridor with her walkin' stick.

'Oh, he's gone down the bookies, with an old friend.'

'Is he bettin' again?' I turned to look at her.

'Oh, good God in heaven no, he's just gone to watch the gee-gees, mun. He won't put a bet on.' She was tryin' to act, but she couldn't. I could see it in her eyes. She looked sad. I noticed again how tiny she was. Her small frame and her jet black hair. She was like a little terrier. And she had a little mole on her forehead. It was skin colour, but it was there. And it 'ad definitely grown since the last time I'd seen her.

'Maybe you can 'elp me actually, I'm tryin' to play draughts on the Internet.'

'The Internet?' I felt too tired to work it out in my head. It was like I was in a dream.

'Well, I 'ad money left to me from Alf's compo see, love, so I went and bought myself a laptop.'

A laptop? I thought. Fuck me.

'Aye, right' I said, 'Ummh, OK, let me 'ave a look. What's the problem then?'

We sat down on the sofa, in the dark, and worked it out together. Peg was definitely bonkers but there was somethin' about her too. Somethin' soft and gentle. I fiddled with the laptop for a bit but the screen was bright. And after a while I got tired.

'Can I put the lights on Peg? My eyes are 'urtin', she nodded and carried on playin' draughts. That was the first time I noticed Flo wasn't there.

'Where's Flo?'

'Uh?' she lifted her head, as if she hadn't heard the question.

'Flo, where is she?'

'Popped her clogs, cofia,' she said matter-of-factly and went back to playin' draughts. I stopped.

'Peg mun, why 'aven't ew told us? When did it 'appen?' She ignored me, and the light from the computer screen made her face look white. 'Peg! Why didn't ew tell me? Or Mam?'

162

She looked at me, smiled.

'Jesus Nelly, if everyone phoned each other every time a dog died . . .'

Somethin' didn't feel right. 'But, you loved her. I thought she meant everythin' to you.'

She popped the laptop on the sofa, between us.

'Sam fach, when you come to a certain age, you understand that 'though things 'urt you, it doesn't mean you 'ave to tell the world.'

'But, but, me and Mam, we would've liked to know. And Gareth.'

'I'm sure you would've. But fuck me, you've all 'ad enough on your plate. It's been like a tossin' well mad house around here recently.'

Peg put her head back on the sofa. It was weird, 'cos I could still smell Flo. And I could still see her runnin' about, shittin' on the carpet in weird places. Peg seemed different to me today. She looked lonely. I didn't like to think that, but it was true. So, I moved the laptop and sat next to her. She smiled and closed her eyes. I really wanted to give her a cwtsh but I knew it would be strange. We weren't really those types. So I made sure my arm and her arm were touchin'. Her reddish cardigan with some stain on the sleeve, and my navy Adidas jumper. They touched, and that was enough.

We sat like that for about a minute, which is a long time in real life. Without the telly on even.

'Why the hell 'ave you come up here then?'

'For tea.'

'To see ewer Dad, you mean?'

'To escape from Mam.'

'There we are then.' She stood up from the sofa, took her time but managed it.

'Tea it is then. What d'you fancy?'

'I don't care really.'

'What about fish fingers?', she asked lookin' at me serious.

'Ummh, no, maybe not fish fingers.'

I looked at her eyes: did she know what she'd just said? No, I don' think she did. But I don't know either. There was a little spark there. Fair play to her for not bringin' it up mind, if she did know about it.

'Chicken kievs then, I got four boxes for the price of five in Iceland today.' I don't think she quite meant what she said.

'Lush.' I smiled.

We ate our supper in silence. I liked that, eatin' in silence. I sometimes liked havin' the TV on mind, but tonight it just didn't seem right. We sat after eatin' the kievs and potatoes and drank some tea. I like this, I thought. Drinkin' tea after eatin', and lettin' everythin' sink down to the bottom of my belly. When I got to the bottom of the cup, I could see that the whiteness of the china was filthy. Not dirty, but tea stained. God, I thought, I wonder how many people have drunk from this mug? How many cups of tea? After I drank the last drop, I turned towards Peg who was holdin' her cup with two hands. And for some reason then, and I don't know why, I asked Peg about Alf.

'I never knew Alf, see Peg.'

She didn't react surprised.

'No, I don't spose you did love. He died when you were, well, I don't know. You must 'ave been . . .'

'In Mam's belly I was.'

'Was ew? Well fuck me pink.'

'Aye. Gareth was around, maybe you're thinkin' about Gareth?'

'Aye, I must be. Come to think of it, I do remember seein' you for the first time – after he'd died – and I remember thinkin' that you looked like 'im, the spittin' image.'

I 'ad to think about that one for a minute.

'But how? I wasn't related to him, at all.'

'No, well that's what was strange about it . . . Mind you, I was up to my eyeballs in valium at the time.'

We sat in silence again.

'Was it horrible losin' the love of ewer life?' Cringe, I thought, don't ask such a personal question. But it 'ad come out without me 'avin' a chance to stop it. Like a sneaky, smelly fart.

'No not really. He wasn't the love of my life.'

I couldn't ask any more. I didn't know what to say. I gulped. I wanted there to be more tea in the cup, for me to sip and move on. What did she mean, he wasn't the love of her life? I tried to push it from my mind but it came back, again and again like last night's fish fingers.

'Oh don't you worry about all that now, you silly little twat.' My God, she's just called me a twat. 'Saw you in the paper.'

'Aye.' She did know then.

'He was the boy we saw in the paper when you were 'round before, wasn' it? When Flo was still about.'

'Aye,' I tried not to look at her.

'It's OK to hurt you know. If you don't let yourself hurt, it'll fuck you up.'

I looked at her. She swore so much, I didn't even notice she was doin' it anymore.

'Alright, ta, Peg.'

'You can love people for a minute even.'

165

God, this was gettin' embarrassin', but the weird thing was, she was right. I had only known Tellin for a minute, or two.

'I was the same, I loved him for a minute, but then . . .'

'Who, Alf?'

'No,' she said, 'what d'you want for puddin? I've got bananas and milk, banannas and custard or custard.'

'Ummh,' I didn't want her to stop talkin'.

'Or, I've got jam too. You could have some custard with jam. Alf used to love that.'

'Ummh, just a banana then please,' I tapped my leg against the leg of the table. I liked the sound of it, so I did it again.

'Stop that fuckin' bangin' will you. I'll get ewer puddin'. We'll eat it and watch *Coronation Street* on the three-piece suite.'

Three-piece-sweet, I thought. Three-piece-sweet.

When she brought the banana in custard over, I didn't have the nerve to tell her that I hadn't asked for custard. I never have the nerve to tell people things like that. And worse still, the custard was cold. She sat down by me and pressed the button on the remote control. Instead of watchin' *Coronation Street*, she put *Pobol-Y-Cwm* on.

'Cheers Peg. How come you wanna watch this? You don't speak Welsh.'

'Don' I?'

Now, I don't exactly know what that meant. She could be bullin', she could be tellin' the truth. I can never tell with Peg. 'Course, watchin' *Pobol-Y-Cwm* just made me think about Nanna. It was weird. I hadn't seen it for weeks, but the same old things were happenin' on it, 'though my life 'ad changed quite a lot. I would be a good character on *Pobol-y-Cwm*, I thought.

Anyway, I thought I'd ask one more question. I could see Peg was enjoyin' 'avin' me here so I ate the custard and asked away.

'Peg, who was that man who came to Nanna's funeral? That Danny Bishop?' But she didn't say a thing. I didn't try again; she'd heard me the first time. Shit, had I pushed my luck?

'Is the custard nice?' Obviously she wasn't mad with me, but she wasn't goin' to answer either.

'Aye, it's nice thanks, Peg, lovely.'

It's fuckin' cold I thought. I felt somethin' on my tongue, it tickled. I tried to get it from my tongue onto my finger without makin' it obvious. I looked at it, while tryin' to look as if I was lookin' at *Pobol-Y-Cwm*. Was it? It couldn't be. It was black dog hair. Flo's hair. How was that possible? I felt sick. I swallowed quickly and tried to forget, watchin' Denzil and some woman talkin'. Christ, if there's anythin' worse than nearly swallowin' a dog's hair, it's nearly swallowin' a dead dog's hair.

Then suddenly, while I was rubbin' my hand in my trousers, tryin' to get rid of the hair, Peg spoke.

'It's none of your business, mind.' It was as if she was in a trance, 'She loved him, very much. You should know that. You've got a right to know that.'

My God, I knew it. It had been starin' me in the face.

'What? Did they have an affair?'

Peg sat up and looked at me,

'D'you seriously think I would've stayed friends with ewer Nan had she been with another man behind my brother's back?'

I didn't understand.

'She worked down Cardiff. Cleanin',' she mumbled. 'About ewer age.' I nodded and she carried on. 'She met 'im,

167

worked for him. Worked for him and his wife.' I nodded and she continued. 'She spoke Welsh, his wife didn't . . . this was before ewer Gramps and her got together.'

'But why couldn't they get together? If they loved each other?'

Peg snapped, 'Because things like that don't fuckin' happen, love. At least, they didn't then. I'm not sayin' people didn't have affairs.' (So they did have an affair?) 'But 'gettin' together' like people ewer age talk about, it couldn't happen. Not back then.'

'Why not?'

Peg turned to look at me and she looked angry. Water filled her eyes.

'Ewer Nanna was beneath him, love. She was beneath him.'

I couldn't understand. I wanted to ask more. They'd obviously stayed in touch though. Beneath him? Why would that be? If they were like each other, if they loved each other . . . And what did Gramps think? What did he think?

'So, what happened then? They kept in touch . . .'

I searched Peg's face, but she didn't answer. She'd turned her head back to the telly and she was engrossed in *Pobol-Y-Cwm*. That was it, I knew it. I'd never get more than that out of her. Ever.

It was really tidy how it happened, as if that-man-Terry knew exactly when the break for *Pobol-Y-Cwm* was goin' to come. The phone rang. Peg had fallen asleep watchin' the telly. Exhausted after tellin' me all those things. I stood up, the phone still ringin' and ringin' and I went to answer it.

'Hello?'

'Sam?'

'Aye, who's there? Dad?'

168

'No, it's Terry.'

'What d'you want?'

'Ewer Mam, she wanted me to let you know . . .'

'I don't care what she says, I'll speak to her tomorrow.'

'No, she wanted me to let you know. She's been rushed to hospital.'

'Wha'?'

'She wanted me to let you know.'

'You fuckin' said that once. Why the fuck 'nyou there?'

'I am, that's where I am.'

'What's wrong? She fallen? She cut herself cookin?'

'. . . It's the baby, Sam.'

I put the phone down, woke Peg and booked a taxi. I felt numb. I shouldn't have shouted at Mam earlier on. I felt dead. I didn't know whether I could cope with this too. It could be the final straw.

'What's up then love?', Peg asked all dopey.

'I need to speak to Mam, after the fight we 'ad.'

I couldn' tell her she was in hospital. She could find out when everythin' was OK again. If everythin' would be OK again.

'Right you are, love. I'm sure you feel like a right fanny for fallin' out with her.'

I kissed her on the forehead, she looked up. I felt like she was a little girl. She didn't know half the things that were goin' on.

'Cheers for the supper Peg.'

'Anytime love, say hello to that Mam of ewers, and to the new cock on the block.'

I left Peg's house when I heard a toot outside. Cock on the block. I couldn't believe she'd even said that. I jumped into the taxi.

169

'Alright, drive?'

We were drivin' away, down the street when I saw Dad walkin' up the street, towards Peg's house. He was out-of-his-mind drunk. Swayin' and trippin' and leanin' against a wall for a rest. Seein' him didn't make me feel anythin'. He didn't know Mam was pregnant, he didn't know anythin' 'cept what he chose to know. Just like the rest of us, really.

Chapter 16

Thank God the baby didn't die. It was just a scare. But the fact that it nearly died made me realise that I loved it, 'though it 'adn't been born yet even. It would only ever be my half-brother or sister, but I still loved it.

Mam was lyin' there in the hospital bed when I got there. She was lookin' weak. Terry grabbed me straight away and said,

'Everythin's fine. The baby's fine, but most important, ewer Mam's fine.'

'What 'appened?'

'Cramps, turned out it were only wind.'

I wanted to smile 'cos it sounded so stupid. I realised then that the Random Fake Death of my future half-brother or sister 'ad made me realise what it was all about. The grief I felt for him or her dyin' when I was in the taxi was different to that which I felt when Nanna died. It wasn't worse, it was just different. It was like the death of somethin' that hadn't had the chance to happen. Surely, that must be worse? And then I felt really guilty . . .

You see, in the taxi, I'd even thought of what would 'appen if the baby would have died. I'd thought that in a way it could 'ave been a blessin', cos Dad would never have to know. And then, if I randomly murdered that-man-Terry, Mam and Dad might get back together some time. Well, that wasn't goin' to happen now, was it? Although, the thing was, I'd moved on from there. I didn't really think they could ever get back together. I suppose it was like a deep-down dream, that was always goin' to be there.

Hospitals smell mankin', weird. And it freaked me out,

the idea that they're not clean. You can go into the 'ospital to get better these days and catch somethin' worse while you're there. The smell reminded me of things I didn't know I remembered. It made me think of Ysgol Gynradd, it made me think of gettin' paracetamol from Y Nyrs in school, it made me feel safe and in danger.

Mam was in a room on her own. I don't know why. She even had her own telly. I wish I did. I walked up to her, I looked at her, all in white she was. Pure, perfect. And her little bump was obvious.

'I'm sorry Mam,' I said quiet.

'Me too Sam, don' think about it now.'

'Good thing ewer fine, and that . . . the . . . ewer belly is fine, innit.'

'Aye,' she said and she closed her eyes, her head against the pillow. I don't know what the 'Aye' meant really. It nearly felt like she didn't want to have a baby. She looked too old to have a baby today. I'd have to look after her more, I thought.

That-man-Terry just looked over, didn't come too close. Thank God. That would've been cringe.

That night, Mam stayed in hospital. That-man-Terry and me went back home. We 'ad to go back in a taxi, together. That-man-Terry 'ad come over in an ambulance with Mam and he didn't want to wake Gareth 'cos of the way he was at the moment. Fair play to 'im. I looked at 'im in the taxi, we didn't say a word to each other. He was an alright kind of guy, I suppose.

When we got to our road, he paid the driver.

'Cheers, drive,' I said and jumped out.

I went to bed that night feelin' like God 'ad given me another chance. As I lay there, stirrin', I started thinkin'.

Thinkin' about Anti Peg and the person she'd loved for a minute and thinkin' about Nanna and Danny Bishop. I was thinkin' deep and nearly sleepin' when I had a text. It was from Maggie.

'Let's go out tom night Sam. Whatyouthink? D.O.T.S.M r inda legionx'

Sounded like a complete disaster, I thought. That bloody band again. But, then I thought, why not? It wasn't as if I'd be doin' anythin' else tomorrow. And more than that, I'd 'ad a lucky escape tonight with Mam bein' OK. I should let my hair down and 'ave a night out. I thought maybe of textin' Arse to tell her to come over, but I don' think it would be her scene. She's more into clubbin' in Cardiff and pullin' boys who think they're chocolate.

That night, I slept like a log, and I didn't even need Classic FM. When I woke up the next mornin', the music from *Pobol-Y-Cwm* was whirlin' about in my head. I don' know why. But that mornin' was a nice mornin', wakin' up and feelin' positive. I was grateful, because you can't control that type of thing. Either you wake up grumpy or worried, or you wake up feelin' good. I had a funny feelin' about today . . .

Chapter 17

First thing that happened was Dad came over. He wanted to see Gareth. Mam was still not back. As I sat there with him, on the sofa, I wanted to tell him about the baby. I was dyin' to in a way, to his face. Is that twisted? Thing is, it was becomin' damn obvious if ew looked at Mam. But men are weird like that, they don't notice.

Anyway, he saw Gareth pop his head around the door of the telly room, and Dad followed him up to his bedroom. Gareth doesn't come out of the bedroom much these days. Only goes to the kitchen and has a quick nose downstairs. He's alright I think, watches telly, plays computer games, looks at 'Ready, Steady, Cook' repeats. In fact, he's become a bit obsessed with cookery programmes. When I went up to see him this mornin', he told me he wanted to be a chef.

'Is it?'

'Aye, don't laugh. I'm serious. It's a really honest job.'

'I'm not laughin'. What d'you mean it's an honest job?' I crumpled up my face askin' the question.

'You know. Honest, clean. Really clean and honest job, feedin' people. Makin' people stay alive.'

I didn't want to ask more. His favourite chef at the moment is Ainsley Harriott. God knows why. I just left him to it. Jamie Oliver's Dad was doin' somethin' on *This Morning*. How come you're allowed on the telly to cook because your son's a famous chef?

'Shouldn't you be in work?' was the last thing he said to me while I was about to leave the room.

'Aye,' I said and left.

I was supposed to be in work; I was an hour late. I

phoned in, told Chief that Mam's baby nearly died and he let me 'ave the day off. He said on the phone,

'Listen Sam, we don't want to have to lose you, ewer a good little worker. But people are startin' to talk . . .'

'Aye, sorry Chief. I promise I'll straighten up soon. We've 'ad a lot 'appen in the family see.'

He changed his voice,

'Love, I know, I do know. But I have to tell you. Next week, fresh start yeah?'

'Aye, sorry Chief.'

'See you tonight.'

And he put the phone down. Fuck, I didn't have a choice now. I'd have to go to work. Mam came back at four and just before she'd come back, I'd opened the cards that were left for me the day before. One of 'em was pink, and two of 'em were from Tellin's family. Well sort of. His Mam 'ad written this bit in hers, sayin' thankew for makin' Andrew our hero and his Anti 'ad written nothin' much on the same card. The second one was from Vicky; it said sorry. I didn't believe her. But fair dos.

When I opened the third, I was shocked. It was from Danny Bishop. A piece of paper slid out from the card. I read the front, and read the inside. This wasn't about the fish finger thing at all. This wasn't about Tellin. In shaky Welsh writin', it just said, 'Rhywbeth bach i ti fynd ar gyrsie, cadw dy Gymraeg di'n fyw.' Somethin' to keep my Welsh alive. I looked at the piece of paper that had fallen to the floor. It was a cheque. A cheque for five hundred pounds. I don't think I'd ever seen so much money. I was confused. I felt used. I felt as if it was a bribe, but I had no idea why I thought that. Danny Bishop was keepin' Nanna alive by tryin' to make sure I could speak Welsh. I don' know either, was that what

175

he was tryin' to do? Fuck knows. I folded the cheque, and put it in my jeans pocket to decide on another day. He must be fuckin' loaded though. Kind too. But mental.

Anyway, Terry went to fetch Mam and when she walked in, she was lookin' right as rain. Pretty too.

'You're home early love,'

'Aven't gone in yet.'

'Oh right,'

'Aye, well we were late gettin' back, weren' we.'

'Aye, Terry and me were thinkin', d'you fancy a Chinese tonight?'

'D'you think that's a good idea Mam?'

'Why?'

'Wind?'

She laughed and rubbed her hand on my shoulder.

'Ewer a funny one aren' you eh? You up for it then?'

'No cheers, I'm goin' out.'

'Are you?!'

'Don't sound so surprised.'

'I'm not, it's, well that's good news. Where you goin'?'

'Chief's band is playin' up the Legion. Chief and Maggie are engaged now.'

'Duw, Duw,' she said and she did this thing with her lips that meant, 'Oh right, well great, OK. You go, enjoy yourself. And find a fuckin' husband while you're at it.'

I went upstairs to see what I could wear. I 'ad a nice black top I thought I could put on, but of course I couldn't fuckin' find it, could I? I looked and looked, threw everythin' on my bed. Then finally, I found it. I put it on, and did my make-up. I ate some beans on toast in the kitchen, standin' up and waited for Maggie to pick me up at half six. I'd told her that half six was a bit early but she'd said, 'No – Chief wants us to be there for soundchck – we can go 4 free thenx'. Fuck knows what 'soundchck' meant but I'd soon find out. When I came downstairs, Mam was standin' on the bottom step lookin' up at me. I had black trousers on and a black top. She said I looked beautiful. Of course, I knew that wasn't true but it was nice of her to say it. When Maggie rang the doorbell, I was ready and Mam asked if I wanted any clothes washed. I felt a bit embarrassed that Maggie might have heard that. My Mam still washin' my clothes for me . . . I said she could take her pick of all the clothes on the floor in my bedroom and did a cheeky smile. She just said, 'alright love', and flapped her hands for me to get out of the house.

When we got to the club, there was this big poster up on the door:

GIG TONITE – DEATH OF THE SALES, MAN!
and PINK FLUID

I hate it when people spell tonite like that, instead of tonight. Anyway, we went in, and I was quite lookin' forward. Maggie said she'd go and see whether she could pinch some cans from the rider. I never knew who the rider was but sure enough, she came back with two cans of Bow. I don' really drink cider, but then I didn't wanna look rude. And anyway, I hadn' even paid for these cans. I sat down with Maggie in the empty room, waitin' to see somethin' or someone. I could hear men talkin' in the spare room where they usually kept the stuff for cleanin' the place. Mind you, if you ask me, that's a bit of a joke, 'cos this place ain't never been cleaned properly. The carpet has gone another colour since years, and it's all sticky. The tables are sticky, but then at least you know ewer drink isn' gonna slide across it and fall on the floor. Everythin' 'as its positive side.

177

We must've been there for at least ten minutes, talkin' when two men came in. One of 'em 'ad a guitar and the other was 'oldin' an amp and an unlit fag. The one with the guitar looked like Kelly from the Stereophonics gone wrong. He was dark, I'll give 'im that, but he looked like he'd been squashed up against his mother's belly as a baby. He thought he was good lookin' mind, which made everythin' worse really. He looked over at us and winked. Wanker.

'That's Grim,' said Maggie.

'Tell me abour it,' I said, gigglin'.

'No,' said Maggie, lookin' a bit freaked out with me, 'That's Grim – the main singer. He's ace.'

Ace? I thought, what a stupid, stupid thing to say, I'd only ever heard that on some American programme – and in Cardiff.

'And who's he?' I looked over at the other one. Wasn' much to say about him either. He was tall, too tall really. He had brown hair, brown eyes and acne.

'Oh, that's Rab.'

'Rabbit?' I'd heard of him, once or twice. Chief's best friend.

'Aye, that's him,' and Maggie lifted her hand and whispered, 'Arigh?' at him. He smiled.

'No need to ask why he's called Rabbit, is there!' I looked at Maggie all knowin'.

'His mother works up the pet shop in Ponty. Lucky he can play tonight actually, he was taken to 'ospital last week 'cos he 'ad an in-growin' hair on his back.'

'What about Chief then? What does he play?'

Maggie looked at me stupid. 'Chief doesn't play, mun. He's the manager.'

Manager, I thought? Why the hell would this band need a manager?

'Oh,' I said, didn't expect that one either. 'Where's Chief then? Isn't he with 'em?'

Maggie looked down, took another sip of her Bow.

'D'know,' she mumbled.

'You d'know?' I think I sounded a bit cheeky.

'No, well, we . . . we . . . argued and then, he's gone out somewhere else, he might come back after. Says he's gone to sort some more venues out for the band.'

'Is the engagement still on?'

'Yeah!' Maggie looked disgusted, 'course it is. What are you on about? Anyway, it'll be nice for me and you to have a night together, talk and things.'

Aye, I thought in my head. But you shouldn't be drinkin' Bow, I thought, bein' pregnant. I hated bein' all judgemental but I didn' like people drinkin' when they 'ad a baby in their belly.

Anyway, as the night went on, we listened to the soundcheck, which I understand now is some kind of practice before the band actually play. Me and Maggie kept on talkin', and it was a bit like the old times, us two havin' a laugh. 'Cept she was pregnant, and I think I've changed a bit. But, although things had changed, for the first time ever, I kind of liked bein' out. It was a real escape. 'Course I thought about Nanna and all the rest of the shit. And I could never shift Tellin either; he was always there, in my belly. I didn' feel twisted no more though, after Peg 'ad said that I was meant to feel like this. I was definitely goin' to see her after work Monday. Defo.

We were on our third can (which is a lot for me) when the bouncer at the door came up to us and said,

'Uh, girls. You with the band? 'Cos if not, ewer gonna 'ave to go out for half and hour and come back, and pay. Right?'

179

I looked at him, nodded, sort of said 'Sorry'. I got up but Maggie pulled me back.

'Aye, we are with 'em.' Maggie shouted at the Rabbit bloke who was busy with his back turned settin' up the stage. 'Rab!' He turned straight away and came over. Fair play. 'We was just sayin', we're with you inwe?'

God, I would 'ave sooner paid than grovel like this. I wasn' tha' desperate, it was only £3 to come in! But that's what Maggie's like, see.

He looked at Maggie, then at me.

'I've never seen 'em before in my life mate.' Cringe. Then, Maggie started laughin'. 'No,' said Rabbit, 'it's fine, mun, they're with us. Least she is,' he pointed at Maggie. 'Don' know who the fuck she is, a friend of Maggie's maybe?' lookin' at me, 'Ah, but she's pretty mind inshe? She's with us too.'

He winked at me and walked away. The bouncer went too. He was 'appy with that explanation and so we could stay. Like groupies. Fuck, I don' think I've ever been so humiliated. I felt like I was a cow bein' bought in an auction, just to get £3 off comin' into a gig.

'Oh! He's a laugh he is,' said Maggie, 'I love Rab I do.' She shouted 'Thanks Rab!' over to him, and he lifted his hand to say 'No worries', but he kept his back turned.

'Cringe,' I thought. I had to say it.

'Oh shurrup, my Mam always says you 'ave to drive a hard bargain. Anyhow, he fancies you, you little minx!' She pointed at Rab and I reckon she said it too loud. He must've heard her. God.

I went all red, hot, embarrassed. I suppose he had winked, and for a moment that was a really nice feelin', but then I realised I didn't really fancy him at all. He didn't do it for

180

me. It was a compliment like, but nothin' more. I just ignored Maggie. She went to fetch some more cans for us and suddenly I was on my own in the club room with the Rabbit bloke. I sat there for a while fiddlin' with my phone. Then, he stood up from the wires and shit, I watched him from the corner of my eye. He'd clocked me, like an animal with his prey. Shit. He stopped what he was doin'. I turned my body away. But shit, he was comin' over. He walked a bit funny too. I tried not to look.

'So, you work with Maggie, d'you?'

'Aye, good guess,' I smiled but I didn't look in his eyes. I didn't wanna give him the wrong impression.

'I'm Rabbit by the way,' he said, and he sat down. Don' fuckin' sit down, I thought.

'I know, yeah, Maggie said. Ewer friends with Chief, inew?'

He smiled, 'Aye, me and Chief go back a long way. Where you from 'en?'

'Here.'

'Duw, no. I live up Ponty way, Graigwen?'

Posh, I thought.

'Oh, right, cool. You speak Welsh d'you?'

He looked at me a bit funny, picked up an empty can and looked at the instructions.

'This stuff does funny things to a girl, don' it! No, I don't speak Welsh, didn' even go to a Welsh school. My Mam's Catholic, went to Cardinal. Why the fuck did you ask that?'

'You said, Duw, before somethin' you just said,' I felt disappointed, although I didn't really know why.

'Did I? Don' know how the fuck that 'appened. Maybe I picked it up or somethin', my other gran's from Ammanford. Dead now of course, but maybe that's where I got it.'

His voice was deep. He was old. I didn't fancy him at all, but his voice was deep, I'll give 'im that.

I felt guilty, the conversation 'ad gotten borin', and I wasn' interested in his answers. Worse still, from the corner of my eye I could see Maggie standin' with two cans, by the door. Deliberately not comin' in. Cow.

'Right,' I said, awkwardly, lookin' at my phone. Someone text me, you fuckers!

'Right, yeah. OK then . . .?' he was fishin' for my name.

'Sam.'

'Sam, I'll see you after, yeah?'

'Aye,' I said, but I didn't really look up at 'im. Maggie was a bitch. Standin' there like a moron. I know she meant well but I really wasn't in the mood.

'Well?' she asked, plonkin' two cans down on the sticky table.

'Well what?' I looked straight into her eyes. I didn't have anythin' to hide.

'Rab?' she giggled, loved it she did.

'Piss off,' I said. And that was the end of that.

We kept on drinkin' mind. It must've been about eight by now. When was this bloody thing startin? My phone vibrated. Wicked, I thought. I looked at it quickly.

'You home for Sunday lunch? I'm makin starter – melon with parm-ham, carbonara sbag-bol and secret puddin, txt me bck. G' It was only Gareth: he had begun to experiment with food in the house now. He said it was good practice for when he'd wanna try for a job as a chef.

'Anyone interestin?' Maggie asked, obviously a bit bored in the club too by now.

I couldn't be arsed to lie,

'No,' I said, 'just my brother.'

182

She looked away, didn't say nothin' and then she turned back.

'Listen, tha' was a big mistake, I'm sorry 'bout it all, I . . .'

She was pissed and she wanted to get it off her chest. But she was pregnant, she shouldn't be drinkin'.

'Don' worry, it's been an' gone now. Over.'

'Aye, I know, but I wanted you to know, I feel like shit about it.'

'Honest, it's fine, everyone makes mistakes,'

'Yeah, but I looked cheap, I don' know what was wrong with me.'

'Nor me,' I said, tryin' to relax the situation. 'Gareth's a minger!'

Maggie laughed but the laughin' soon turned to cryin' and typical, just as people came to pay by the door, walkin' into the club all fresh eyed and ready for music, I was sittin' with Maggie, holdin' her hand. Her wet hand, wet with stupid, drunken tears.

We got over that little wet patch and the night picked up. Maggie told me that Grim and Rabbit were pissed off 'cos they were headlinin' but that they knew that a lot of the crowd were comin' to see that Pink Fluid band. Supposedly, they're from Llanhari school and they sing 'alf their songs in Welsh. I told Maggie, I didn't see what the problem was but she just said that bands who sang in Welsh always had television cameras followin' 'em.

'Not because they're good,' she said, 'but because they sing in Welsh.'

Supposedly, there was a camera comin' out from some company tonight, 'bout nine o' clock. To do with some programme.

'Don' worry,' I said, downin' another gulp, 'we'll dance to Death of the Sales thingy,' Maggie smiled.

'I bet you will, you minx,' she played with her hair, 'mind, you'll 'ave your work cut out.'

'Why? I'm not that 'ammered.'

'No, it's not that. The Death, well, they're hardly a band you can dance to really, are they? We'll have to mosh. Headbang like.'

Shit, I hadn't texted Gareth back and so I did.

'Aye, I'll be there. Nice one. Mam k? Sx'

I didn't get an answer all night. Gareth wouldn't give a shit how Mam was. Or maybe, he would give a shit if he gave himself two minutes to think, 'cos he's always too busy worryin' about himself.

All of a sudden, the whole place was full of people. It wasn't packed, but it was OK. I was sittin', mindin' my own business when I saw Maggie wondering off somewhere. Probs gettin' us another drink. Pink Fluid came on. Really young they were, but they 'ad attitude. I was quite enjoyin' them. The funny thing was, I think they were singin' in Welsh but you couldn't understand it anyway. They might 'as well 'ave been singin' in any language goin'.

I stood up after a bit, and sort of moved a bit to the music. I wasn' exactly dancin', but swayin' like. Only when I'm pissed, I thought, only when I'm pissed. Maggie had been ages, I thought I should go after her, or at least phone her. But as soon as I had the idea, I felt someone tap me on the shoulder. Shit, I thought, it's Rabbit. I turned around and saw this young man, weedy, in tight jeans and a little shirt. Definitely gay, I thought. He shouted in my ear.

'Hi! I'm lookin' for people who can speak Welsh? D'you know if anyone here does?'

I looked at him funny, up and down. Why would he want to know?

'Umh, I do. A bit.' Twat! Twat! Why did you say that?

'O great, diolch ti, der ffor' hyn!'

He dragged me by the arm and soon enough I was in front of a big, black fuck-off camera. The boy in tight jeans went over to this very good lookin' man, who looked a bit like Mike Phillips the rugby player. He smiled, did a thumbs-up sign.

'Be' 'di denw di?'

'Sam ydw i,' I said. My God, they were gonna ask me things in Welsh. On camera. And I was hammered. Think, I thought, think of all those Welsh words. Bara brith – ga i baned o de? – Cerddoriaeth – joio – mwynhau – ydy – cwl. I knew I was goin' to, I was goin' to fuck it up and not get things out. Die on camera. Die, die, die!

'Gret, diolch ti Sam. Dw i'n mynd i ofyn cwpwl o gwestiyne i ti oce? Am y band, oce?'

'Ym, ie, iawn, dim problem,' I said.

He better ask some easy questions. Shit, shit, where was Maggie when I needed her? Where the fuck was Maggie?

'Nice and snappy oce. Atebion, nice and snappy!'

Get the picture I thought. I'm happy with nice and snappy answers. I'll only be able to manage one-word answers anyway.

'And ar ôl pump . . . Sam, pam wyt ti wedi dod allan heno?'

Ummh, shit, shit. Why am I here? Why the fuck am I here?

'Dwi, dwi yn hoffi cerddoriaeth.' I was sweatin' like a mule. Duh, nice one Sam, you like music! Great answer.

He carried on, 'Yn y cefndir mae Pink Fluid, wyt ti'n hoffi'r band? Ydyn nhw'n chwarae'n dda heddiw?'

'Ydy,' I said, but he stopped me.

'Gret, gret, ond paid edrych at y camera, edrych arna i.' He smiled. What a prick! I'd been starin' at the camera, not at him. 'Na i ofyn eto, paid a phoeni. Ydy Pink Fluid yn chwarae'n dda heno?'

'Ydy,' I said. Die, die. I want to die. 'Maen nhw yn swnio'n da iawn. Mae Pink Fluid yn cyffrous.' Stop there, I thought, quit while you're ahead, but I didn't did I? I fuckin' didn't. 'Ond ti dim gallu clwed geiriau nhw o gwbl. Mae 'The Death' fod yn da hefyd. Nhw ar olaf,' I smiled.

I didn't care how many more questions he was goin' to ask, I wasn't goin' to answer them. I was so chuffed with myself.

'Gret, oce, diolch ti Sam.' He shook my hand, fuckin' stunnin' he was. Whoever was his girlfriend, in Cardiff somewhere, she was lucky.

I left the camera crew feelin' really chuffed with myself. A bit high in a way: I'd managed to do an interview in Welsh. First time I'd spoken it for yonks. I went straight for the back room where Maggie 'ad disappeared to get our cans. I didn't knock, I just popped my head in through the door. I shouldn't have. Up against a wall with no trousers on, was Maggie. Grim was stickin' 'imself into her and she was shoutin'. She didn't see me, and I'm glad. I didn't say nothin' to her either. It wasn' any of my business. I just felt sorry for the baby in her belly who had to hear all this goin' on. And I felt sorry for Chief. How come she could regret shaggin' my brother but she couldn't stop herself doin' it again?

I walked from there and back into the darkness of the gig. It was cool, I was enjoyin' walkin' about on my own. I tried not to think about Maggie naked in the little box room, but it just jumped back in my head all the time. I didn't feel angry with her anymore. I kind of felt sorry for her. Pink Fluid had finished and there was just background music on. I could see that the camera crew were startin' to pack up their things. Then I thought I need to know when the programme's on, so I can tell Nanna. I couldn't believe it, for a moment there I thought she was still alive. So, for the sake of it, I went up to them again. I must admit I was a bit worse for wear by then.

I pushed past some people and went up to the good lookin' one, the boss. He was talkin' to a girl with a tight ponytail. I could hear them.

'I know, I know, we will get time. It's nine now, cariad, we'll get to Cardiff by 9:30 and grab something there love. La Boheme?' he kissed her. God, I was jealous. She said something then,

'But, I'm starvin' and, Christ . . .'

Her smell was familiar, lovely, hauntin' me. I stopped them in their tracks.

'Sori, fi eisiau wybod pryd bydd y rhaglen ar y teli?'

The director smiled. The girl in the ponytail turned to look at me. I couldn't believe it. I knew that smell was familiar. It was Dwynwen. Dwynwen the girl that wanted me to do more Welsh things in work. She smiled, she looked awkward.

'Dwynwen?' I said, 'Oedd fi ddim gwybod oedd fe'n ti.'

She smiled, she looked embarrassed, I don't know why. The man looked at her surprised.

'Shwt ych chi'n nabod eich gilydd te?' How did we know each other?

'Y Comisiwn', she said.

He nodded his head, as if to say, 'Right, I understand now,'

'Bydd y rhaglen ymlaen Nos Iau nesa', diolch ti Sian.'

Sam, I thought. Wasn't Dwynwen goin' to correct 'im? But she never. They both smiled at me. Thursday night it was then. Funny she didn't want to speak to me too.

As soon as I'd turned my back on the camera crew I saw Chief. He looked flustered, a bit mental actually.

'Hi Sam, love. 'Ave ew seen Maggie?'

'Umh, she went to fetch us some drink,'

'Right,' he said, 'which way did she go?'

I didn't know what to say, but suddenly from the smoke and the dark, Maggie appeared, lookin' right as rain, holdin' two cans. They kissed and that was that. They must've texted in the meantime then, because they didn't look as if they'd been arguin'. Maybe Maggie had made that up. I don't know. I don' really understand them two, but it's nothin' to do with me. Maggie smiled at me.

'Alright?' she gave me a can, and I said thanks with my eyes. She didn't look guilty or nothin'. It was her I saw in the little box room wasn' it? I started doubtin' myself.

Half the crowd 'ad gone by now, like Maggie had said would 'appen. But Death of the Sales, Man! still came on and made us all deaf. They were fuckin' awful, I couldn't believe I'd said they were good on camera. I'm sure they were better than this in the soundcheck, I thought to myself. Oh well, who gives a fuck if I've said they were good on telly? No one means anything they say on telly anyway. It's all an act. I drank more Bow. It was startin' to turn on me actually.

The Death played for ages. Me, Chief and Maggie stood together and watched. Chief liked the idea of bein' the manager, I could tell. The Grim boy, who looked like Kelly from the Stereophonics gone wrong, was there for us all to see, singin' 'is little face off. And yet, Maggie didn't look as if nothin' 'ad 'appened. Maggie and Chief started whisperin' and then Chief turned to me. He shouted in my ear, so loud that my ear was hurtin' and sort of ticklin' from the sound,

'So, I hear you've been gettin' on good with Rab . . .'

I looked at Chief, and did a 'fuck off, this is sooo borin' look. He smiled. I liked him. He was protective of me, I think. Chief and Maggie held hands and I held my Bow.

Twelve o' clock everyone started leavin'. There was a fight outside and all the bouncers ran after these two blokes. I love seein' bouncers run through lots of people. I love it because they love it. You can tell it's what they've been lookin' forward to all night.

I was ready to go home now, but Maggie and Chief 'ad other ideas.

'I'm goin' now,' I said, smilin', 'Thanks for gettin' me in free.'

'Oh, wait a bit more will ew?' Maggie was so irritatin' sometimes, she was tryin' to play cupid, and she was bein' so obvious about it.

'No, serious, it's late, I'm goin'.' I started walkin'.

'No,' said Chief, and he seemed to mean it, 'We'll walk ew.'

I couldn't say no. But, as I knew would 'appen, who came with us? Rabbit. It was like watchin' a shity cheesy film, with no excitement. I tried to get myself excited, I really did. Someone liked me, it was obvious. But the problem was, I really didn't like him. Not like that anyway.

We all walked.

'You live up Ponty,' I smirked at Rabbit. 'Ewar goin' the wrong way if you wanna go home.'

'The night is young,' he said. He'd been sweatin' like a

pig on the bass guitar but the funny thing was, I hadn't noticed him at all on stage. Bad sign, I thought.

'Maggie said you were in the paper this week,' he said.

Maggie and Chief were walkin' in front of us. They quickened their step and laughed a bit.

'Oh, it's a long story really. Not interestin' either.' Bitch, I thought. Why the fuck did she tell 'im tha?

'Haven't you got to help the boys put things in the van or somethin?' I tried my hardest.

'We're leavin' our stuff there tonight. The Grim is fucked, off his face. KO'd in the toilets. Spew all over the shop.' He laughed. I really didn't want to know that.

And weirdly, the word 'spew' made me think of my jeans. Shit, my jeans. The cheque in my jeans. I bloody hope Mam hasn't washed them . . . I scrambled for my phone . . . Rabbit looked at me funny . . . I dialled home . . . waited . . . ringing. Ringing again. And then someone answered.

'Hello? Who's there?'

'Gareth, who's there?'

'It's Sam, mun!' I said, all frustrated, 'Is Mam still up?'

'Course not. What do you want?'

'Will you go to the washin' machine?'

'Wha'?'

'Just fuckin' do it,' I shouted at Gareth. I felt guilty about swearin' at him and I also felt a bit shit for swearin' in front of Rabbit. I looked up to see whether he was listenin'. Yep. He definitely was.

'Alright, I'm here. Now, what the fuck is all this about? Are you steamin?'

I made him look through the clothes in the washin' machine, and sure enough my jeans were in there. Check the pockets, I said. Check the pockets. But I knew there was no point. After rummagin' for a while he said he'd found a washed-out piece of paper. He thought it could have been a receipt or a cheque maybe?

'Alright,' I said, flatly, 'Don't worry. Cheers Gar.'

I couldn't be bothered to explain to him, so I hung up the phone and popped it back in my pocket. That was that. Nothin' I could do about it now. I sighed deeply, nearly cried. But I didn't.

'Everythin' alright?' asked Rabbit.

'Sorry?' I turned to look at him, 'Aye, aye, you just reminded me to check somethin', that's all.'

And then, without me expectin' it, he put his arm around me. He really liked me, I could tell. And he thought, with me bein' cold, that I was playin' hard to get. But he was wrong, I was tryin' to play impossible to get. He stopped me on the street, and it started to rain.

'Wait a minute,' he said. He was so tall, I looked up.

'It's rainin', what are you doin?'

I didn't have no choice, he came towards me. His big dry lips. Came towards me. Nice shaped lips, but dry, mind. And then he just snogged me. I snogged 'im back. Not 'cos I wanted too, but because I didn't want to hurt his feelins. 'Cos after all, he was alright. Then after about a minute, he stopped kissin' me. His tongue was the last thing to come from my mouth. I wasn' used to attention like this. His kiss 'ad been nice tho'. I felt safe with him, not blown away, but safe. Maybe that's how ewer supposed to feel, in real life.

'Are you seein' someone?'

I paused. Thought.

'I was, sort of, but not anymore.'

'Can I see you again?'

'Alright.'

191

Why did I say 'alright'?

'But only if you tell me your real name.' I didn't mean it playful, I just couldn't type Rabbit next to his number on my mobile. It would be cringe. Kinky even.

'It's Richard' he said, completely matter of factly. No game, no flirtin', no mystery. And all I could think about, as I smiled back at 'im was . . . No. That would be tellin'.